ORIGI

NEW WRITING F...
BRITAIN'S OLDEST PUBLISHER

Risk-taking writing for risk-taking readers.

JM Originals was launched in 2015 to champion distinctive, experimental, genre-defying fiction and non-fiction. From memoirs and short stories to literary and speculative fiction, it is a place where readers can find something, well, *original*.

JM Originals is unlike any other list out there with its editors having sole say in the books that get published on the list. The buck stops with them and that is what makes things so exciting. They can publish from the heart, on a hunch, or because they just really, really like the words they've read.

Many Originals authors have gone on to win or be shortlisted for a whole host of prizes including the Booker Prize, the Desmond Elliott Award and the Women's Prize for Fiction. Others have been selected for promotions such as Indie Book of the Month. Our hope for our wonderful authors is that JM Originals will be the first step in their publishing journey and that they will continue writing books for John Murray well into the future.

Every JM Original is published with a limited-edition print run and bespoke cover designed by an up-and-coming illustrator from Liverpool John Moores University. This means every time you buy one of our covetable books, you're not only investing in an author's career but also building a library of (potentially!) valuable first editions. Writers need readers and we'd love for you to become part of our JM Originals community. Get in contact and tell us what you love about our books. We're waiting to hear from you.

JM ORIGINALS

She That Lay Silent-Like Upon Our Shore

Brendan Casey

JM ORIGINALS

First published in Great Britain in 2023 by JM Originals
An imprint of John Murray (Publishers)
An Hachette UK company

1

A CIP catalogue record for this title is available from the British Library

Trade Paperback ISBN 9781399801577
eBook ISBN 9781399801584

Typeset in Minion Pro by Manipal Technologies Limited

Printed and bound in Great Britain by Clays Ltd, Elcograf S.p.A.

John Murray policy is to use papers that are natural, renewable and recyclable products
and made from wood grown in sustainable forests. The logging and manufacturing
processes are expected to conform to the environmental regulations of the country of
origin.

John Murray (Publishers)
Carmelite House
50 Victoria Embankment
London EC4Y 0DZ

www.johnmurraypress.co.uk

I

It were cold in the mornin first I saw Levi thrashin agin the edge of the world – mind, she werenoh calt that then, and I didnoh know her sex. I thought she were a beast, like me; a great glistenin beast stretched belligerent-like across the earth, knowin well she had no right to be here, cep the one she force upon it.

I bin livin in the old abandoned bothy for the past long while cause it were quiet there and I were left alone. It were peaceful some, cep for the rookery of seabirds what squawked like the devil every time I passed. More oft than noh, I squawked back at em and flapped mine arms the way they did me, cep they used their wings a course. It pleased em none when I did that and they squawked harder and created a godawful din as though I were the cheekiest thing they ever saw. I tolt mysen noh to squawk at em so, that is the way of birds I sayt to mysen, still it couldnoh be helped – soon as they started up, I squawked right back at em. A child I am, like that.

I were growt wild, but that is the only choice a soul has in the Wastes, as this part of the Quag is knowt. The Quag is an island, it is the world, more or less, beyond which there is nought cep sea and sin, where everythin drops off into the Great Abyss or Darkness – or Hell as it is otherwise knowt. It is calt the Wastes on account of the fact it is rocky and infertile but also cause it is unconsecrated and godforsaken and the like. The Wastelands, its true and proper name, were anythin beyond the limits of the village. I still wore the clothes of those what lived there but had growt some in the long while I bin out here, so things were gettin scant in the arms and legs. The boots were no more-an flaps of leather what were bound and kep agether with twine – I couldnoh afford to discard em though, for I'd freeze out here without em, sure and certain. It were fortunate I'd lost a considerable amount of fat, so widthwise the clothes sat upon me fine so.

I were raw-boned on account of the fact I were half-starved from a fierce sparse diet of fishes, rotted fruit and stale bread. More oft than noh – due to hunger and impatience – I guzzled the creatures raw, the bones half chokin me as I wolfed em down. Our waters teemed with fishes for we was an isolated island and our people ate nothin what come from water black as Melas – which is what the sea is somespells calt on account of the fact she were so dark and all. Anywise, souls believed it unclean, they sayt anythin come from water black as that couldnoh come through God. Moreover, they sayt the water stretched to the shores of the godless and were polluted with sin, they sayt the sea become black from the wicked tryin to wash their burnin skin free of sin. It is best to point out that I'm noh responsible for the keck and blether other men believe. Anywise, the water were bitter cold and it were scarce

2

I went in further-an my knees. I waded in with the spears I mysen had fashioned and were now quite handy with, hittin my mark more oft than noh. I were qualmish about puttin mysen into Melas' cold dark hands, but hunger will make ye do things. Ye will be pleased to know my legs ner caught fire nor wasted away in that cesspool of sorrow and vice.

I musta appeared a rare thing in my fine clothes turnt to rags, spearin fishes with the trousers rolled to the knees. My hair were growt and knotted, and my face caked in filth, but there was none out here to look upon me, and I woulda cared none should there bin. The long scraggy down on my face growt in patches for it couldnoh yet grow proper – I were a boy becomin a beast were what I tolt mysen. I imagined I were becomin somethin fierce and untamed and this pleased me no end, for it were what I'd allway wanted – to be wild and fierce and free. It were true that I had strange notions bout mysen.

For all my fierceness and freedom I were hungry some, that were for sure and certain. I'd taken to eatin the wispy thing-a-ma-gims and do-gacks what growt spindly and frail from inbetwix the cracks of the rocks. Inland, back from the Sheers, I gathered blewits and lousewort just as the women and weans done in Grathico – which were the name given to the village by the God-fearin souls what built it. The rotted fruit and stale bread I collected every next day from the old crone what lived on the outskirts of the village, apples and plums she left, the saplins of which bin brought with us on the ships from Ereb, though that were in the aforetimes a course, afore my wee naked and gory sen bin birthed into this barren and blighted skerry. The crone left the basket out back of her shed so as I could come and go as I pleased and noh be seen, nor she suffer shame or punishment for her act of kindness. I'd noh have survived without her, for it werenoh just food she'd given but blankets and tinderboxes and other such worldly effects what would sustain a soul in the Wilds.

So that, more or less, were what I were up to, I were off to see the old crone on account of the fact I were fierce hungry. I didnoh like doin this much, as it meant I had to leave the Wastes and go back to the village – the thoughts of which made me liverish and queasy. Grathico were situated on a steep with the Prelate's house way up top near the cliff while the other huts and bothies staggered down the slope as though the island itsen were tryin to tip the village and all its souls into the sea. From the gates the township rose up afore ye like a cross what bin half raised for crucifixion, for that were the shape it bin built so as to remind souls of the configuration of atonement and salvation. At the heart of the village stood the church with its spire what reached up to the heavens, twort God Himsen, that most Holy Bein what presided over the fallen souls of Grathico. Outside the church were the square where markets happened and Grathicans bartered and haggled. The limits of the village were a large rectangle what enclosed the cross wherein the crop were growt and animals were kep and grazed.

The crone lived right at the edge of Grathico so I didnoh have to venture in far, still-yet, after bein away for such a spell I allway felt fierce jittery about returnin – noh from fear mind but betrayal, to mysen and the Wastes as, truth be tolt, I were startin to nurture a fair amount of affection for my new state of savagery. I felt somethin akin to pride twort the neediness of my body. I liked how it ached and burnt most the time, kep me alert so it did; a creature stalkin the Wastelands were how I saw mysen, though praps my brain were just turnt to mush

4

from malnourishment and the like. Anywise, it were becomin more difficult to leave the Wastes, and my loathin for the village and himsen the Prelate were growin stronger – if that were possible.

When first I left the crone seen me lurkin round with the hangdog eyes, like as noh she'd heard my stomach rumblin from behind her shutters. Anywise, next thing I knowt baskets of slops was bein left very sneaky-like out back of her shed, so I started sidlin up to em – sniffin round some like a dog for his dinner. And this time were no different; seein the basket in its usual spot I approached very slow and cautious, once I were there though I begun stuffin food into my gob and pockets like there were no morrow to come.

'Tis a fenny-miry mornin, ainny?'

I near lep out my skin when she sayt that – it were the old crone hersen, in the flesh like. She musta slipped out from inbetwix the stones of the shed. She'd ner spaked to me the wholespell I bin out here, truth is, she werenoh spose to.

'Tis fierce squelchy like.'

When she sayt that she were talkin bout the weather. I sayt noh a thing but stared at her, gormless and silent. The crone were in a state of undress, her clothes bin throwt agether in a hurry and her wimple fixed slantwise – the grey hair were half up, half down with loose strands what kep fallin across her eyes and squigglin down her face so as she had to keep pushin it out the way – I spose there bin no time to fix hersen proper afore leavin the house to pounce upon me. She leant agin the shed and I could see her wrinkly old arm were part bare cause she'd noh done the buttons what ran underside her sleeve – this seemed to nettle her none, for these old ones donoh feel the cold anywise. I werenoh accustomed to seein

5

the bare arms of women, so it had me distracted. There was dark spots all over it and the skin were loose and swung back-a-fort when she moved – it turnt my stomach some, truth be tolt. Seein me lookin, she tried to cover hersen best she could, but her arm were still there and all.

'The day clings to me,' she wheezed, as though befelled by some great tragedy.

Ha! The day clings to me! I bin in the Wastes so long I almost forgot such sayins, it is true though, here the weather wraps itsen round ye like a sodden pissy blanket. They are poetic these people in the way they talk, somewise poetry has seeped into their tongues without gettin into their blood.

The crone gazed up wistful and forlorn into the nasty old clouds waitin for me to say somethin. When naught arrived she lost her nerve and I saw her eyes slide sneaky-like and skittish twort me.

'Aye it is,' sayt I, finishin whatsoever were in my gob. ''Tis squelchy fenny, tis fierce squelchy fenny, wouldnoh thee say, mam?'

I spaked in a voice what were too loud and she looked at me queer and nodded her head, unsure of hersen, or mysen. In a sudden the fear had creeped into her and she turnt to walk away without sayin nothin more.

'I'd say it might lift later, mam,' sayt I to the crone's back. 'The day will unwrap itsen from round thee so it will. Thou shalt be set free and all!'

Her shoulders clenched at the sound of my voice, her pace quickened as she scurried inside and slammed the door behind her very frightened sen. I knowt she were peepin on the further side of those curtains, so I looked down at the food awhile afore makin a show of turnin my back upon it and walkin away. It werenoh so brave a gesture as all that cause, truth be tolt, there werenoh much left in the basket on account of the fact that what werenoh in my pockets had already bin guzzled and were sloshin round the belly.

I decided I'd noh return – I'd leave the crone's slops to rot good and proper in the basket, she could give em to whatso-ever animal they was intended. Now I were proficient with the spears I didnoh need her, nor her filthy vivers. Way I saw it, she werenoh actin out the good of her heart – these peo-ple ner do. Aside which, it were the last thing what bound me to the village and I needed to cut that tie, till I did I'd ner truly be a thing of the Wastes. It is man's dependence on other men what enslaves him, what dispirits him. That is rule number one in *The Philosophy of the Wastelands* which I have just now decided to compose for mine own amuse-ment. Mostspells, I think I'm very clever, till I mind how dozy it is to think such a thing, then I can start feelin very sorry for mysen – truth be tolt, I can get fierce wound-up if I think hard upon mysen.

II

I come back through the Wastes, what were all grey and bleak and the like. It were rock for the most part, large smooth stone what ye had to climb over, with boggy swales inbetwix. The Wastes were what I imagined the moon might look like, I pretended that somespells, that I were livin on the moon and all, and the wee annular light in the sky were in fact the Quag floatin round in the great black ocean of the night – old Melas hersen stretched across the sky. From my crater on the moon, I'd stare down upon the Quag and imagine I could see the wee tiny spec of a beast-boy sittin upon some lonesome rock – poor thing. I'd wave to him and all. *Howbe?* I'd say. *Don't envy ye down there upon that godforsaken isle – keep the chin up though, and if ye ever have the time and means, come visit me on the moon someday, thou wouldst be most welcome.*

Anywise, comin twort the bothy, I saw the hasp were loose and the door wide open. I thought it were the wind at first, till I heard rummagin round inside. Comin down upon my knees, I scurried along the ground till I reached the window-sill from where I peeped inside.

'Hoy!' bawled I, risin to the feet and runnin to the threshold. 'Hoy! Scat!'

A goat were stood inside, nibblin on oddments what bin left upon the table.

'Out! Git!'

She turnt to look upon me as though I were the one what should explican himsen – *What's thou want then, eh?* sayt she. These goats roamed the Quag and were sayt to bin here since afore the Prelate and his kin ever set foot upon it. They were a skewbald and hairy lot – the goats that is – what with the fringe comin way down past the eyes and all. How they saw aught were beyond me.

'Mmmmeeeehhhh,' sayt she, afore turnin back to her meal of rare and inedible things.

I recognised the goat for she had very particular markins upon the snout. Noh long after I'd come out to the Wastes I'd managed to catch her, as I had notions of usin her for milk the way they done in Grathico.

'Thou shalt provide me with milk!' declared I, like a commandment from the heavens – very satisfied with mysen I were.

Next mornin though I wakened to find one end of the rope still attached to the bothy while the other were become all tattered and goatless – *Thanks for the sleepover and all beast-boy but I have become bored and am goin back to my cullies forta roam the Wastes and bleat my skull off.* Didnoh blame her truth be tolt. There were a whole herd of em what strolled by every-now-a-then, up there in a distance, upon the rocks noh far from the cave, and it were her what allway stopped to look

9

upon me – *There he is lads, tried to keep me tethered to that tumbledown pile of sticks with a rope – mooncalf!* Then they'd all bleat emsens dozy laughin at me – swear to God.

Anywise, it were the same goat tormentin me. I had to come in behind her so as to manoeuvre her slat-ribbed and bony sen out the bothy – *No rope this morrow mooncalf?* enquizzened she, very brazen as she trotted out the door.

I grabbed one of the spears I'd made especial for fishin and headed twort Melas, for now the baskets of slops were at an end I'd have to be fierce vigilant if I werenoh to starve all agether. Comin to the top of the cliff where her dark and glittery sen stretched out afore me, I spied a small figure walkin along the sand in the next cove. He were hurlin things at the sea, and I knowt it were a whelp from the village come to throw the Sacred Stones. I'd growt fierce protective of my ground in the Wastes and were nettled to see a Grathican so close – Stone Throwers werenoh spose to come this far, and it were scarce that I caught sight of em.

Scurryin along the cliff I scampered down the rocks to the shore. The boy were way out in a distance where the sea met the sand; it looked as though he were about to disappear into the spindrift of the ocean – that or be consumed by the waves what bit down fierce and relentless upon the Quag. Approachin from behind, so as noh to be seen, I studied his wee serious sen. He were swaddled in the knee-length black smock what were the Stone Thrower's garb; upon the feet he wore wine-red boots made from worked goats hide, dyed and treated with tormentil root. All souls in Grathico had a particular dress – the Stone Throwers, the Closemen, the Fowlers, the women and the weans. Garms were kep immaculate and worn with regard, for the dress of a Grathican were an outward display of the spiritual constellation of the soul what lurked within.

10

The boy helt his body rigid, cursin and such, for he were filled with righteous indignation at the dark unruly waters.

'Geh thee back Unholy Darkneth! Devilish Blackneth! Watersome Beastht! Take thee back to himthen the Devil! Git!'

He were pluckin stones from a hessian poke what were secured across his chest, it bin stamped with the symbol of the red cross, the Prelate's beaked mask crucified upon it. I watched the arc of the stones as they left the boy's hand but heard em none as they broke the surface, for they was drowned out by the great susurrus of the sea. Melas swallowed the stones without a sound, hidin em in her vast and shadowsome body like they was the Host what himsen the Prelate doled out to the gapin black maws of the God-fearin at church. The Stone Thrower kep shoutin even after the stones left his hand, he punched the air and spat in triumph when they hit the water – derivin much pleasure from the untolt damage he were doin upon the evil spirit of the sea.

The stones was meant to keep Melas at bay so as she did-noh swallow the Quag whole in the middle of the night, so that she didnoh creep into the village while it were sleepin and smother its souls with her dark and dank sen. The sea nettled the Prelate no end, kep him awake at nights, tossin and turnin in his sheets – a great torment to him, so she were. It were for this reason boys was sent into the Wastes to throw the Sacred Stones – to temper and tame her. The child afore me were very wean and hadnoh bin a Stone Thrower long. Stone throwin were only for whelps, boys werenoh allowed to touch the stones afore their eighth year and beyond their twelfth they were deemed too old. This lad were a zealot though, ye could see it in the way he helt himsen, thrustin his wee arms at the sea, shakin his fists and cursin her.

11

'Howbe?' whispered I, to the back of his skull.

He turnt some, lookin down the sand, unsure whether he'd heard aught over the roar of the ocean, thinkin praps a spirit of the Wastes were hushperin to him. When he turnt back to the water I creeped upon him some more. Puttin my hands behind my rump, I leant into him.

'Howbe?' enquizzened I, loud and sharp.

Leppin into the air the boy dropped the stone what were in his hand and spun round to face me. It were my turn then to come back in surprise, for the face of the child were disfigured. Aneath his neb, in the shape of a wee beard, the skin were all raw and mottled, it were knotted and knarry with welts weavin through it what looked like a score of white spiders crawlin twort his gob. Clutchin the poke to his side, his frightened and skittery sen sayt noh a word as – keepin his eyes upon me – he bent down to pick up the rock. Droppin it into his sack I heard it clicker-clatter agin the others what were inside.

'I greeted ye,' sayt I.

The boy sayt naught but pressed the poke closer agin his side as though I were about to relieve him of his precious stones.

'I've no interest in ye wee rocks, if that's what nettles ye.'

Naught, cep the susurrus of the sea.

'Did ye think a spirit of the Wastes was come for ye?'

I looked out at Melas who were fierce angry, spatterin and roarin and the like despite the pacifyin effects of the stones.

'They seem to be doin their job donoh ye think?' sayt I, noddin at his poke. 'The sea looks to be cowerin afore their very heady powers – crawlin back into hersen, all sorrowful and repentant and the like, wouldnoh ye say?'

'I know ye,' sayt he, spittin words in a sudden. 'Ye *are* a spirit of the Wastes. Ye are godleth. I'm noh bidden to thpake with ye.'

Godless were what he meant, noh godleth, the boy sayt his S's a wee bit strange, all hissy as a snake and slurred some.

'Seems godless noh to acknowledge yer own kinfolk or address an elder so familiar-like.'

'Ye and I are noh kin, yer kin are the beasthts of the Wastelands, those what roam out here on four legth or belly. Ye are the kin of beasthts and wilderneth!' sayt he, regainin some of his nerve.

'I cannoh argue with that,' sayt I, puckish as-ye-like. 'What ye say is truth itsen.'

The boy made to move around me.

'I see ye are First Stone Thrower,' sayt I, juttin my chin at the insignia upon his chest. 'Thou seems too wean for that.'

There were only a dozen Stone Throwers at a time, one of which were first or head of the others, this were allway the oldest boy, the one closest to becomin a man.

'God and Prelate didnoh think so.'

'Has himsen the Prelate managed to convert the ocean yet?'

'If he so wills,' sayt the boy, avertin his eyes and tryin again to pass me.

'I only spaked with ye to warn that ye should go no further – the weather has shifted the rocks makin crossin to the next sand treacherous.'

He paused to think some.

'I will go inland.'

'Ye are noh permitted ado that, well ye know.'

'I will go and see the rockth mysen.'

'Do as ye please, it will be a long trip for naught. Mind though, this is noh yer country, ye are unfamiliar with it and it is hostile twort ye.'

'I've bin blethd.'

13

What he means is that souls leavin the village to go to the Waste-lands needs be *blessed* by himsen the Prelate. The Bindin Words will be sayt over em and they will be given a vial of consecrated soil to carry agin their hearts. Holy water will be placed upon the eyes, lips and ears and the three prayers will be recited. These protection spells only last a certain while afore they begin to wain and a soul risks succumbin to the treachery of the spirits what roam there. It is sayt the Wastelands and the demons what inhabit it have a charm unto emsens, their sorcery is powerful and can seduce a weak soul into dissolution and lechery. Himsen the Prelate says the Beast has the voice of a woman and can sing songs so wicked and enticin they can paralyse a soul if it is noh vigilant. Grathicans who wander into the Wastelands without first bein blessed meet an excruciatin and torturous end – their skin begins to rot and blood will come from the eyes and the unfortunate soul will burn from inside out. Somespells as punishment souls are taken into the Wastes to be consumed alife by the demons what inhabit it. First they are bound to the pole and covered with a sheet what has bin blessed, then they are carried deep into the Wastes where the pole is fixed to the ground and the sheet is stripped away from em, whereupon all the imps – the tiny devil-weans of the Wastelands what live in the shadows and underside the rocks – attack the wretched soul, leavin their small teeth marks deep inside the flesh of the sinner.

Most souls of the village had ner witnessed this punishment as it werenoh bidden – by all accounts it were a hideous and fear-makin thing to watch a man welter and shriek on a pole as the very soul were burnt out of him. Somespells, if the wind were right and the sin particular and great, ye could hear the guttural animal cries of the wretch whose life couldnoh leave him quick enough. All Grathico would become silent then, listenin to the wind as it whispered distant agonies through our wynds and narrows.

14

The bodies of these unfortunates was placed at the north, south, east and west of Grathico. They was placed at each point of the cross to remind souls what happens to those what succumb to temptation or defy the word of God. More oft than noh, the weans of the village would gather to throw stones at the bodies as they hung limp and haggard from poles. I mind one child throwin stones at the body of his own lifeless father – it took some goadin and all, but after a spell he helt the rock in his wee tremblin hand and, very tentative-like, throwt it at the battered carcass of his own flesh and blood. A cheer went up among us weans, our fists shootin into the air with glee, so the boy throwt another, and soon he had a taste for it and we others couldnoh get the stones to him quick enough, such were the frenzy he were in. All the weans, mysen included, shouted and egged him on, and afterward he were carried upon our shoulders like he were the wee king of Grathico. As we carted him off, hallooin and jeerin and chantin, I caught his mother skulkin bout the corner of mine eye – when she noticed me lookin, she lowered her skull and scurried down the narrow what wormed its way back to the heart of the village.

The stench of these rotted souls and the incense what were swung over em wafted through the village for weeks. It is mine estimation that bein half beast mysen is what protects me from the imps and demons of the Wastes – they donnoh devour their own kin is what I expect.

'Ye have come all this way, which is further-an ye spose to,' sayt I to the Stone Thrower. 'Ye still have to make it all the way back. It is my calculation that the blessin what protects ye will wither afore ye has the chance to reach the safety of the village, which means yer wee Stone Throwin soul will wither with it.'

He seemed to think hard upon what I sayt him afore raisin the orbs to glare upon me.

'I know ye,' sayt he. 'Prelate hath tolt all about thee, thou lives outside the grace of God. Thou hast stolen from the sacristy of the church. I know all ye have done – the fires of damnation are stoked and tended for thee, a thpecial place in Hell await those what kill their kin.'

I kep calm and wouldnoh satisfy the child by risin to his words, for I were used to the accusation and well versed in turnin the cheek upon it.

'Best stop smirkin child, thou art ignorant and wersh and thy mouth precedes thee. Mind too that we are alone out here and there is naught to protect ye, and if it is true as thou says, that I murder mine own, it stands to reason I'll noh hesitate to commit the same upon a deficient whelp such as ye.'

He sayt naught to that but blinked the orbs as though he'd become frozen inside his body.

'Thy mug has become all red,' sayt I, 'cep the wee white and creepy beard ye has there.'

He stood mute with the fists clenched, till I made a lunge at him and he turnt and scuttled up the shore.

'There is plenty of sea to be pacified the way ye come,' bawled I, but he didnoh acknowledge my words, 'I too throwt the Sacred Stones as a wean! Think ye hard upon that!'

He slowed when I sayt that, pausin a spell afore marchin on.

It were true what I sayt him – I mysen had throwt the Sacred Stones as a boy, amusin some to think upon it, all things considered. I were sent into the Wastes like other weans, I liked wanderin over the Quag on mine own, even though I were scared some. The Sacred Stones I just kinda throwt very sluggish and lackadaisy at the sea, I didnoh shout and howl at her like a mooncalf but just looked at her, for Melas had allway managed to cast a spell upon me. To be honest with ye, my heart were ner in the throwin of stones.

16

III

The two conversations with Grathicans had me kittled and surly for I'd noh spaked to another soul the wholespell I'd bin out here. Suspicious the crone should approach me and the Stone Thrower be out this far in the Wastes, I decided to visit the ships which were where I went to mull things over, especial if I were in a mood, which were oft enough, truth be tolt. As I walked along the shore, the gulls squawked in circles above and I tolt em to shut it for a soul couldnoh think amid such din.

'Shut thy squawk-holes,' sayt I.

They didnoh listen.

I jabbed the spear willy-nilly into the sand – bit sulky-like, on account of my mood and all. Soon though I begun pretendin I were usin the spear to prod bodies what lay there, checkin to see if they was still alife or whathaveye. After proddin em I would have to step over em on account of the fact I'd started to imagine I were no longer walkin across the shore but through a cave what were all creepy and drippin with water, which werenoh water at all but poison or the like. I had to dance round the drips otherwise they'd bore a hole right through my skull. The reason I kep goin through the perilous and unwelcomin cave were cause there were a fierce allurin and feminine creature what were awaitin me at the end. I wound my way through the twists and turns of the cave by followin her beguilin voice what sounded day and night in a quiver-makin, mournful song. Thing were though, ye couldnoh listen to her too long otherwise ye'd fall into a deep sleep from which ye'd ner wake. Anywise, I had to cram the fingers into the lugs every-now-a-then so as I didnoh fall prey to her dwam-makin voice. The souls I were steppin over and proddin with the spear were the bodies of men what bin unable to control emsens and had succumbed to the creature's intoxicatin song. It were sayt that she hersen were impossible to seduce but that were cause she'd ner come across a fierce wild beast-boy afore and, while it upset and frustrated her, for she were a proud and untamed soul, it were inevitable that she would yield to my fierce brutal and charmin ways – poor thing.

I'd stopped at some stage to sweep sea curdle from the shore, it were fierce squishy with mottled colours of browns and greens and blacks. I liked how it felt betwix the fingers, all slimy and spongy and the like. I'd taken to eatin it as well, boilin it in water and puttin it in the gob, noh too much though as it sent the belly burbly and rankled. Anywise, I'd grabbed a great lump of it and placed it atop the skull, pretendin I were the fierce allurin creature of the cave with long lustrous hair and all. I were quite feminine about it, truth be tolt, sweepin it from the mug and out the orbs and so fort.

The allurin creature hersen were just about to swoon into mine arms when the din from above become loud and broke my train of thought. *Mooncalf!* squawked the gulls. *Thou art a dozy mooncalf with sea curdle atop thy skull!* Turnin skyward, I watched the birds circlin above and took a deep breath of salt air. The reek of Melas' fecund and brackish gizzards were for allway in my neb, constant-like, smotherin all other scent. Since comin to the Wastes the tang of brine ner left the gob, causin it to become dry and claggy. Melas were ingrained in the flesh, in the blood too I imagine, like as noh, her cool and watery sen flowed through my veins and swirled about my heart. The sea had possessed and tenanted my body like a spirit – God's truth.

Anywise, in a distance the ships come into view – all forlorn and jagged they sat, charred and half submerged in the sea. I quickened my pace some but kep the sea curdle atop the skull just cause I felt like it and forta spite the gulls. These ships were the same what had brought the Prelate and his kin to the Quag a course, delivered em from the turpitude into which Ereb had sunk. In the early years, after they'd arrived, there'd bin murmurs of sedition among a faction of followers. Upon bein discovered the dissidents tried to steal away but were caught afore they could set sail. In front of all the village the ships were burnt and scuppered as a warnin to any Grathican who were thinkin of turnin agin God and his people. It were also a declaration to His Most High and Holy Sen of the unflinchin commitment of the villagers to forge His will upon the Quag – Grathicans would remain on this rock, His glory on their lips till the last.

The burnin of the ships were commemorated in the Affirmation ceremony which marked the date the founders had first set foot upon the Quag and proclaimed it God's dominion. On the seventh day of the seventh month each year, a parade were marched through the village whereupon Grathicans become a great mass of bodies and incessant prayer. The Prelate were at the helm a course, holdin part of the mast from one of the ships high above his skull – the mast bin preserved and kep in the sacristy of the church as one of the sacred chattels from the Old World and time of Exodus. Grathicans were tolt how after the destruction of the ships the seditious souls were taken back to the village afore bein doused in animal fat and set alight. Ablaze and in flames they were chased from the Quag – the shriekin from their gobs guidin em into the cold black arms of the sea.

Effigies of the dissidents were made by the women and the weans – straw and twigs was bound agether with twine and fashioned into wee human figures. At the end of the ceremony they were lit and throwt from the cliff; hundreds of burnin effigies sailed over the edge of the Quag as line after line of Grathicans moved fort to swear allegiance to their God.

I'd come down the year afore to watch the ceremony from the shore – creepin all sneaky-like and silent over the rocks even though it were impossible for Grathicans to see or hear me. With the belly pressed agin the damp and swarty mull, I'd watched the burnin effigies fall into the dusk, watched em light up the dark and explode in fiery shards agin the rock. Some burnt out or disintegrated, the smolderin ash of twiggy arms and legs featherin their way down the heugh. It were mesmerisin watchin the cliff become fluid and molten, cascadin twort the sea. I'd a nostalgia for it, truth be tolt, which I were conflicted bout, sure and certain. I minded well runnin wild as a wean with the others, heart thuddin, fire whirlin round my skull as I thrust wee flamin effigies of the dissidents into Grathican mugs and whooped like an imp of the Wastes.

Anywise, durin my time in the Wilds, I'd come oft to look upon the sorry-lookin ships. When first I arrived I'd waded out to em in the low tide, squelchin through Melas' gelid sen till I reached the creakin mass of their hulls. As a wean the ships had allway seemed like a distant relic or sarsen; in my mind they'd become a livin thing lurkin in the gloom of the sea. Close up though they were ancient and fragile – creakin and moanin in the shallows, lamentin their subjugation to the craggy foreland of the island.

The wreck of the first ship were like enterin a cave. Waist-deep with the sea, I'd waded through its dark and creepy innards as birds fluttered above, escapin into the light what penetrated the hull and cut through the thick, salt air. Inside the hollow of the wood every movement were amplified, my breath reverberated agin the hull, makin it sound like the ship itsen were breathin. As mine eyes adjusted, I'd seen a large shape hangin from the centre of the upended hull. Corpse-like, it swung on its axis like the bloated body of a sea creature hung by its tail, slowly spinnin round its own mortality.

Comin closer, the form took shape and I saw it were a clinker-built yawl hangin by a single davit what had become trapped betwix a fissure in the hull. Bow pointin seaward, it twisted and creaked some, moved by a force I couldnoh detect. After much fuss and bother I'd managed to cut it loose and we two fell into the arctic blackness, the slap of its frame ringin out in the cavernous ruin of the ship.

Pushin from the stern, I directed it out into the light and checked the wood for warpin or damage. Bilge water were creepin up its hull and it needed repairin but, all in all, it were in good shape. Bringin it to the other ship, I tied the yawl to the wreckage and climbed aboard to gather bits worth salvagin; a few plates, a battered salver, cutlery and other odds and bobs. From the quarterdeck I'd prised a compass from the rotted wood – to what ends I couldnoh say, for what meanin has a compass when ye have no bearins in the world? My favourite spoil from the ships were a spherical object made of brass. It were intricate and heavy in the hand with strange shapes and symbols marked up-a-down it in a language I didnoh understand. I couldnoh be sure of its purpose but thought it were somewise used to read the stars and yer place within em.

Usin my coat like a sack, I'd loaded the booty into the yawl and brought it to shore, whereupon I begun draggin it down the sand so as it were nearer the bothy. I hatched a plan to sail my wee bony and unseasoned sen to distant lands where there were no such thing as Grathico or Prelates and where, more like than noh, a fierce allurin and feminine creature awaited me. Haulin the boat were heavy work and I had to rest every-now-a-then. Crouchin inside the wee hull I shouted and jeered at pirates and the like what I imagined were sailin too close and were, no doubt, intendin to climb aboard and take possession of my ill-gotten spoils. After catchin my breath, I'd climb out again and drag the wreck further down shore.

I kep the yawl in a hollow at the base of the cliff, covered with shrub and twigs so it couldnoh be seen. The compass and the star-readin instrument were tied in a pouch and hidden within. Ye are the only soul what knows it's there a course, and it goes without sayin ye'll keep it to yersen.

Anywise, sittin upon the shore I pondered Grathico's history as it teetered in the shoals, slowly succumbin to Melas' dark and tetchy sen. The ruins of the ships had come to mean somethin to me, they'd become a symbol of sorts, I guess – a stubborn and broken beacon of freedom and captivity.

I'd given up tryin to fathom what the Stone Thrower and crone were up to – ye'd be at naught tryin to figure the whys and wherefores of Grathicans, for that is an endless puzzle of infinite permutations and best left to souls divested with more patience than God has bestowed upon me. Pausin a spell, I wondered whether there might be a *Philosophy of the Wastelands* somewhere in all that but, truth be tolt, I didnoh have time to think upon it as Melas were on the ebb and it were time to fish, for there were a rock from which I liked to spear what become half exposed in the low tide. Asides which, if ever I try to think hard upon somethin I usually end up thinkin bout everythin else cep the thing at hand. For example, if I say to mysen, *Take thee to the ships and mull over such and such*, I end up thinkin bout fierce allurin and feminine creatures or Grathican history or the like, anythin cep the thing I'm spose to – tis fierce frustratin, truth be tolt.

I rolled the trousers up the pegs and waded into the water, headin for the rock upon which ye could stand and wait for the fishes to swim by. They was skittish creatures fishes, and could turn quicker-an a blink and dart under rocks or disappear into the endless dark of Melas' vast and murky sen. Ye had to be fierce patient and still forta catch em and I were neither those things, so I'd spent a longspell cursin the heavens afore I managed to catch one. In the end I begun concentratin on the fish's spirit, what I believed helped some – that sounds fierce dozy I expect, but such are the things what occur to ye when ye are half starved and on yer ownsome.

Pullin a fish from the water, I watched it wrigglin upon the end of the spear – writhin and foldin its spangly sen back-a-fort upon the metal what impaled it. *Aaarrrrh! That is fierce painful*, sayt the fish, *why'd ye go and do that then?!* It become still a spell, then started threshin the tail about with the gob and gills openin and closin as though it were tryin to draw breath from the water what no longer surrounded it – *Out all the fishes in the sea, ye had to go and gore my flesh – typical!* sayt he, unbelievin his great misfortune. When he stopped wagglin I took him from the spear and placed him upon the rock, then I went back to standin still with the fishes swimmin back-a-fort aneath me – unmovin I were, an old statue atop the rock amid the dark and moody expanse of the sea.

There were a whole tribe of fishes millin bout under the surface, turnin this-way-a-that. I had mine eye on this one lad what had winked at me with the scales when he turnt and were caught in the sun. Afore I could spear him though the whole lot disappeared, scatterin to all parts of the sea without me havin so much as moved a muscle. None too impressed, I raised the skull and saw things had become still and eerie. The gulls was quiet and Melas hersen had become hushed and unstirrin. With the hair bristlin on the back of the neck, I lowered the spear to my side.

Pppppppppffffffffffffffffff!

The sound near toppled me from the rock. Castin the orbs about, I scoured the black water till I spied a glittery mist waftin slowise back to the surface of the sea. I stayed still, starin at the spot where the water bin disturbed, waitin for what may happen next.

Pppppppppffffffffffffffffff!

This spell the sound come through my body, I felt it in the belly and saw the whole thing – sea hurled into the heavens afore comin back to the surface, fierce laggard and feathery. I couldnoh see what it come from, it were as though the sea itsen were exhalin, as though the ancient black lungs of the world had exhaled after holdin its breath since afore the beginnin of time – which is a good longspell, I expect.

24

Pppppppppffffffffffffffff!

I sallied from the rock, sloshin through a gaggle of kelp and sea curdle what become wrapped round my pegs. Comin ashore, I headed straight for the cliff – *Hoy!* sayt the fish I'd left atop the rock. *Hast thou noh forgotted somethin? Thou hast put a hole through my side and abandoned me forta rot!* Scutterin to the top of the cliff I stared across Melas but saw naught cep her dark and undulatin waves bobbin up-a-down, laughin at me she were – *Thou art a scared rabbit!* sayt the sea, amused at my quiverin sen.

I waited in vain a longspell, till back twort the horizon the Leviathan come burstin from the sea. Launchin her great and hefty sen clear out the water she showed me the long white expanse of her belly, which I took to be some kinda challenge or slight, for who knows how such creatures spake – *The belly gowk!* she were sayin. *What's thou make of that then?!* I watched as the Great Fish arched her back, hangin there a spell afore comin upsy-down upon the shadowy surface of the brine – *Wack! Bosh, boshshsh!* come the sound of her body agin the water. *I could crush thee betwix the spine and the sea should I want. Thou wouldst noh know up from down, should I come upon thee,* sayt she, afore the water parted and she were taken back into Melas' dark and gapin maw.

Standin atop the cliff with the gob open, I become a mute mooncalf what couldnoh move but stood gazin upon the black and watery divide what concealed her, what kep her hidden from the world. I were become divided mysen from havin seen her; I were elated some, though at the samespell felt as though somethin had bin taken from me, like my gizzards was a ball of twine what had become tethered to her tail and part of me were bein dragged with her into the shadowy depths of the sea.

25

IV

I come back the followin day to wait for her return. I'd decided to sit atop the cliff till the Leviathan again raised her great and mysterious skull forta glare upon the world of man – *Ye lot still here? Right, I'm gonna flash the belly, then it's back to glidin through Melas' dark and unendin depths, undisturbed by human mischief.*

It seemed cruel that to catch her breath she were forced to enter a realm to which she didnoh belong and where she were made vulnerable to the cunnin and guile of man. It were true she coulda bin more delicate about it and noh brought attention to hersen by leppin from the water and rappin her great mass agin the sea. I spose that's why it were calt breachin, when a creature such as her trespasses into our world – it were a transgression agin the usual order. I sat there imaginin her body risin from the water over and over – sheddin the dark afore thrashin hersen agin it. *Neither ye realms hold me!* she were sayin. It were an act of defiance, or so it seemed to me – the breachin of the Leviathan were an assertion of pure will agin all probability, it were an oblique declaration from the darkness.

Anywise, it were while I were sat there ponderin the mysteries of the world and willin the Leviathan to rise from the sea that I heard footsteps crunchin through the Wastelands behind me. Afore I had the chance to turn and see who it were, Withy had plopped his long ungainly sen next me and near frightened me into the grave. I were startled, sure and certain, and we two stared upon each other a spell – him musterin a smile and me all taken back and aghast.

'Didst noh hear me over the din of thine own very profound and prophetic thoughts,' sayt he.

'What's thou doin here?'

I were tryin to come across very calm and unruffled, when in sooth my heart were beatin like a trapped rabbit poundin its thumpers agin the chest.

'Stretchin the pegs. Do ye think I sit around Grathico all day waitin for ye to return?'

'Ye can do as ye please,' sayt I.

I heard somethin rustlin in a distance and turnt to see a dumpy figure stumblin twort us. He were wrapped in a white sheet what were helt snug about the chin with the wee round mug peepin out like a shrivelled old mother. I looked at Withy with a squishy enquizzenin expression.

'The sheet has bin blessed,' sayt he. 'His irritatin sen insisted upon it. His own sen were blessed and then the sheet too forta wrap around him – a double blessin – mooncalf.'

'Is that he?!' bawled the Sheet in a distance.

'A course it is he, does thou noh have orbs?'

'Is it noh a spirit of the Wastes in his form?'

'Art thou noh a gowk in the form of a shrunken blather-spakin ditherskull?'

The Sheet begun shufflin twort us.

'Stay there! I will spake to him alone a spell.'

'That werenoh agreed upon.'

'It werenoh unagreed upon neither – stay there,' sayt Withy, a wee more affable.

'I donoh want to stand here on mine ownsome!'

'Stay!'

Turnin back to me, Withy rolled the orbs.

'Tis unlike ye to carry the spear, Withy,' sayt I, eyeballin the weapon in his hand.

'Tis unlike me to roam among the spirits of the Wastes.'

'The spirits of the Wastes arenoh concerned with spears, as ye yersen once tolt me.'

'Tis for peace of mind,' sayt he, shruggin the shoulders. 'Are ye noh interested in knowin what I bin up to since ye bin gone from Grathico?'

'I expect yer bout to inform me,' sayt I, lookin round to see if there were others.

'I prowl the Fens.'

'What?'

'I prowl the Fens,' sayt he, glarin upon me.

Beyond the village and the fields were the Fens what were a kind of bulwark betwix Grathico and the Wastes – a no man's land separatin the God-fearin from the godforsaken. Fens come from the word fence I think, noh fens as in wetlands, or fenny as in marshy and damp, I think it bin shortened by the lazy gobs of Grathicans, but I'm none too sure about that, and nay bother anywise. I knowt well what Withy were alludin to and didnoh appreciate it bein brought up.

28

'Why art thou spakin upon the Fens now?'

'It were ye what started it, what with yer talk of spirits and spears, asides we ner spaked upon it back then.'

'The time has past,' sayt I, startin to rise to the feet.

'Fine so,' sayt he, placin a hand upon me, 'we'll leave it be.'

Withy had bin my guardian as a wean, he'd taken me hither-thither, raised me more or less when the Prelate werenoh about. There'd bin a time when the two of us were near inseparable – through the weantime and beyond. He'd helped shelter me from the whims of the Prelate. Swoopin in with his long and gangly limbs, sweepin me from the house and out of harm's way. Withy were also the town crier, it were his voice what rung through the wynds and allies of the village forta tell souls when to church or when to clear streets or whatsoever decree need be proclaimed. He didnoh spake but sung the proclamations – truth be, if God could sing Withy were what he sounded like, the tongue of that divine spirit had somewise become loose from its skull and crawled inside the gullet of mine oldest, dearest and most estranged cully.

The Sheet, or Throstle as he were properwise knowt, were a master craftsman, though he might noh have appeared so upon first sight. Like as noh, it were his hands what had fashioned the boots worn upon the Stone Thrower's feet. Workmanship and craft were important in Grathico; aside prayer and worship, labour were seen as the closest means of doin God's work, though a soul allway had to keep the sin and fallibility of man in mind. It were for this reason imperfection were woven, hammered or forged into all things – a sign of deference and humility afore the perfection of His Almighty Sen. Throstle had taught me a thing or two about leatherwork, about tailorin too, I'd bin handy enough with the awl in my day – which werenoh long ago, truth be tolt.

29

Throstle were also knowt to be the Prelate's drudge, and spent his spare time runnin after him, fetchin him this-a-that and tendin to his every need. He'd bin given the name Throstle for his diminutive size and also for the fact of his bein a flutter-tongue, blatherin and chirpin away in the manner of his namesake. Both Withy and Throstle had spent many hours in the house of the Prelate and I'd growt with em allway around. They bickered like two old ones but they was close, noh like Withy and I bin, but still they was close.

'Thou doesnoh seem radiant nor cock-a-hoop to see me.'

'Why art thou here?' enquizzened I, bit short like.

With these two in the Wastes, I knowt, sure and certain, somethin were awry. It werenoh Withy's usual disposition to be all jovial and the like, it seemed forced and unnatural, especial in the Wastelands. Slidin the orbs out to sea I made sure the creature hadnoh returnt.

'To see ye,' sayt he, turnin the skull to the ground, very despondent and all he were.

'To do his biddin,' sayt I. 'The Prelate has sayt the prayer over ye has he noh?'

'How else could I move through the Wastes?'

Turnin back to the sea, I become silent and sullen.

'I watched ye from a distance, glarin upon the water as ye are now. What do ye expect to gain from starin at it so?'

'Naught do I expect from it.'

'That's noh true,' sayt he. 'Ye expect somethin from it, I can tell by the way ye was loomin over it and all.'

'I were loomin over naught!'

I'd become agitated again but tolt mysen there were no point lettin Withy's gangly sen rattle me none, for it were best to be calm and find out why they was here.

'Can I come over now?' enquizzened the Sheet.

'No!'

'When?'

'Soon!'

I could feel Withy's orbs upon me as I stared upon the sea.

'Right,' sayt he. Sighin like a child, he rifled through his pockets for his pouch of blend.

Tappin the pipe agin the back of his hand, he filled the bowl and placed it in his gob.

Grathicans smoked a mixture of dried mullein and mugwort, and one or two other ingredients what they made a great fuss to keep secret. The herbs were dried and ground with a pestle or in the palm, dependin how ye liked it. Withy sayt any soul what ground his blend with a pestle were scatter-brained and dozy and should be throwt from the edge of the Sheers. He were fond of his pipe which he believed nourished the velvety lilt of his voice.

'Do ye have light?' enquizzened he.

'Thou knows well I have no light.'

He shrugged and I watched him fumble round the pockets for his tinderbox. It were pristine and polished for Withy were a fastidious creature, especial with his smokin rig. There were a round of glass on the lid but he preferred to use the flint and strike. Usin short spills he transferred the flame to the bowl of his pipe and drew hard upon the blend with great pleasure and affectation. I kinda tittered at him inside the skull, I couldnoh laugh out loud for I couldnoh let him see I were relentin any. Withy were a character, so he were, and it were true he amused me some.

'Looks uninvitin to me,' sayt he, juttin his chin at the water.

Placin the tinderbox upon the rock he slid it sneaky-like twort me.

'Looks brawny and fierce to me,' sayt I. 'Tis unrelentin, and I respect that.'

He made a humphin sound in the back of his throat what I took to mean he were somewise mockin me.

'Blasphemy where ye and I come from.'

I put my hand over the tinderbox and slipped it into my pocket.

'It is sayt ye eat the fishes raw from her dark and polluted sen.'

'Why art thou here – in sooth?'

'The sea is risin,' sayt Withy, starin hard upon the horizon. 'Melas is engorged and swollen further.'

'Blather-spake! I watch her day upon day, she is unchanged.'

'Prelate says Hell is comin north, just as it moved upon Ereb it is now marchin upon the Quag.'

'Hell and damnation are his concern, and ye poor souls of Grathico.'

'Tis yers too, will allway be.'

Withy turnt to look upon me with the orbs very serious and grave.

'The Beast moves within it.'

'Again?' enquizzened I, curious in a sudden with the lugs pricked and all.

'The Beast circles the shores of the Quag.'

'What beast?'

'There is only one – the Devil, Leviathan, his shadowsome sen in the sea.'

'Blather-spake.'

'Souls have witnessed it.'

'What?'

'Souls have witnessed it lurkin neath the skin of the sea, blowin its wrath into the welkin. It is sayt a trail of dead fishes is left in its wake, their bellies turnt to the sky.'

'Prattle,' sayt I. 'Hast thou seen it?'

32

I felt a twistin in the guts knowin others had glimpsed her.

'Nay,' sayt he, 'I've noh.'

Withy gave me a very weighty look.

'Hast thou?'

'What?'

'Seen it.'

'Nay, Withy, I've seen no Devil in the sea. Dozy thou hast become.'

'Art thou sure?'

'A soul would mind such a sight,' sayt I, smirkin and tryin to seem very amused by such haver and gibberish. 'I'll keep an eye though, thou wilt be the first to know should I come across the Beast. How does it look, this Devil in the sea?'

He turnt from me, drawin upon his pipe and starin at the water.

'It is sayt ye are in communion with the seas and have summoned the Beast to our shores. It is sayt ye have calt it from these cliffs, that ye know its tongue and have brought it to the Quag forta destroy the house of God.'

I looked upon Withy as though he were derangement itsen.

'Thou believes it?'

'Ye cannoh live out here, thou knows. Prelate willnoh allow it.'

'He has till now – why's that?'

'Thought ye'd perish, I thought ye would.'

'Havenoh.'

'Thou art skin and bone,' sayt he.

'Thou spakes?!'

'Aye,' sayt he, titterin some, 'though that is my form.'

The thing about Withy were, he were very tall and spindly – he were abnormal in his heighth and width for there were

33

naught on his bones on account of him bein so long and all. He were fierce gangly, sparse diet of raw fishes and rotted fruit or no. Spindle-shanks I calt him, he were none too smitten with the name but I calt it him anywise.

'Thou looks poorly.'

'I've growt fierce is all,' sayt I, bit huffy, truth be tolt.

'Thou wert allway.'

'Truth,' sayt I. 'Truth itsen.'

'Fierce what though? I were ner sure.'

'Fierce me.'

Withy snortled to himsen.

'Aye, sure and certain, fierce ye.'

We took to bein silent then, starin upon the water while Withy puffed away at the pipe.

'Ye live in yon crumblin bothy?'

'Aye, ye know it?'

'Noh till recent, let us go there.'

'Why?'

'It were made by the hands of men, it is safer-an out here.'

'How long dost thou have?' enquizzened I.

'That depend on ye.'

'How so?'

'We're spose to bring ye back by gloamin.'

'I'll noh be goin back, Withy.'

'Well I know,' sayt he. 'Let us go to the bothy, a storm is comin.'

I rolled the orbs. Withy believed he could somewise commune with the sky and that it had chosen his very bony sen from all God's creatures to whisper its secrets. To be fair, he were none too shabby at aururin the weather, still-yet he'd bin knowt to be wrong a good few spells as well.

'Come on so,' sayt I, nudgin him, 'raise thy long and forlorn bones.'

Slowise, he rose to the feet and we turnt the heels twort the bothy where I now lived.

'Did ye tell him bout the sea comin forta drown the Quag?!' enquizzened Throstle as we come past.

'Aye.'

'Did ye tell him about the Beast what has bin seen lurkin there?'

'Aye, Throstle, quiet.'

'Did ye tell him the Prelate says he has become a spirit of the Wastes and spakes the tongue of the Netherworlds?'

'Shut it!'

'Did ye tell him lest he comes with us he shall be strung to the pole and burnt alife?'

Withy stopped walkin and turnt to Throstle, who closed his gob and stared upon the ground.

'Thou looks a mooncalf in thy sheet, Throstle,' sayt I. 'Is it in mine honour that thou hast swaddled thysen in bed clothes?'

He shook the skull and I stared into his wee round mug with very arched eyebrows what tolt him I werenoh convinced, whereupon he turnt away all agether.

'I have missed ye, Throstle,' sayt I. 'I have pined for ye in the long desolate hours of mine exile. I have calt upon the lonesome stars in the dark and cryptic night forta bring thy sheeted and fearsome sen to my side.'

I waited till he cast the nervous orbs upon me.

'My prayers have bin answered.'

Throstle put the head down and shuffled silent-like along-side us. I slipped Withy a furtive wink and watched the smile he forced wither and crack as he turnt from me and marched on.

V

The sun were well past meridian and had begun throwin its long shapes and shadows across the sparse barrens what had become my home. Throstle looked about himsen as though every sound were a spirit comin out the shade to swallow him. Raisin his right hand to his mug, he helt the heel of his palm over his gob while his arched fingers lay splayed across his cheeks and forehead like a many legged creature had attached itsen to his face. This were the symbol of the mask what were used in Grathico as a greetin and to show allegiance to the Prelate but also to protect a soul from inhalin the spirits of the Wastes, for it were thought that even its replication might somewise protect ye.

It amused me to watch Withy and Throstle's very jittery sens squirmin through the Wastelands and so I begun dancin round like a mooncalf – sidlin up to em and teasin em some, for although I were anxious they was here, I were giddy all the same – a sign I'd bin in the Wastes too long, I spose. Music begun to sound in my skull and I become scampish and dozy. Withy werenoh disposed to my behaviour and shimmied away from me as though I were a great embarrassment to him – so I moved closer, snugglin into him brazen-as-ye-like. I begun circlin him, whoopin and shoutin and wigglin the body about. Withy knowt me well and had witnessed such buffoonery on my part afore – though ner in the Wastes a course. Truth be, I think he enjoyed my strange mood but wouldnoh show it, for bein insouciant and aloof and the like were his only settin. In general, it seemed a rule of his noh to laugh or enjoy himsen but I saw he were smilin as he turnt his skull to draw on his pipe. He were attemptin to hide his mirth as though it might give the wrong impression, as though it were somethin unworthy and shameful, but he were smilin some, sure and certain – it musta bin a terrible burden upon his very serious sen.

'Thou art touched,' sayt he.

'That's right, Spindle-shanks, I have become deranged!'

In the end, just to goad him, I jumped upon his back and he begun coughin and splutterin, tryin to shake me off like he were a wild horse or the like. Throstle mumbled somethin I couldnoh understand on account of the fact he were still makin the sign of the mask.

'Remove thy hand from thy mug, puffin! I cannoh fathom a word thou says.'

Puffin were an insult what were, for the most part, weanspake, it were near every next word what come out their gobs and were considered the heighth of disrespect. I think it come from the fact they considered the puffin to look particular and dozy – poor creature. Anywise, Throstle lifted the hand a tittle but didnoh remove it.

'Thou shouldst stop with the clownin,' sayt he, through the fingers. 'This is noh the thing.'

'Tis noh the thing?! What is the thing, Throstle? That is a question I am most keen to answer!'

It werenoh long afore I could see Withy were becomin sullen in sooth, so I jumped down from him afore his mood turnt black all agether, which is best to be avoided for he can keep himsen miserable longer-an any soul I ever knowt and, truth is, I cared noh to endure his glum and moody sen, skulkin round and draggin his feet as though he were a child and so fort. Titterin some, I spun round to face him but both he and Throstle were lookin the other direction and had become dead still and silent. Walkin over to see what had grabbed their attention so, I saw half a dozen figures standin in a distance starin straight upon us.

'The Closemen.'

'We can see that for oursens, Throstle,' sayt Withy, nudgin him away with the elbow for he'd become snuggled right up agin his side.

The men were stood on a small hillock, wearin the dark hooded habits with the large red cross upon the chest. The First Closeman pulled the hood back from his skull and the others done the same. Still-as-ye-like they stood, hair flappin in the wind, hands in the pockets with the sternest mugs they could conjure.

'They come with ye?' enquizzened I, slantwise from the gob.

'Brought us to the bothy but ye werenoh there, then partway to the cliff till we could see ye. I thought they'd gone back to Grathico.'

'Stayed to keep an eye.'

'I thought that's why ye was here, Throstle,' sayt I.

He turnt the skull to me, much offended.

'It is best noh to go alone outside Grathico. Prelate bade me join Withy, asides I can help sing us through the Wastes if our protection spells begin to wither.'

I scoffed at that but sayt no more.

Withy made the sign of the mask to the Closemen but they didnoh return it. I stared upon em fierce-like till I couldnoh help burst out laughin. Their faces changed none, as though noh registerin anythin, like they was statues or replicas of men. My belly started to churn and I begun to feel incensed, standin there watchin em starin upon us with their big gloomy sens, tryin to be all intimidatin and the like.

'They're here to keep an eye is all,' sayt Withy. 'Let us go.'

'Aye,' sayt I, smilin some, 'soon.'

The music what had bin in my skull were changed – it become slower and drawn-out, like the hummin of insects what were interrupted by a great crashin. *Hhhhummmm* and *crashshshsh, hhhummmm* and *crashshshssh* were what sounded in my skull, then two short crashes – *hhhummmm* and *crash, crash, hhhummmm* and *crash, crash*. The music put me in the mood for a bit of Thrum-Patter, which were a worship dance done in Grathico. What ye do is, ye keep yer hands agin yer sides and kick the feet out, stompin upon the ground and turnin slowise as ye go. Ye can also do wee skippin kicks or grand leppin kicks – there were also wee sideward movements ye could do with yer feet, swingin em out some without takin em off the ground, but that is a tricky step I'm noh able for.

Walkin out some, I scowled at em what were in a distance. Takin off my coat, I handed it to Withy who werenoh movin but starin gormless-like upon the men.

'Donoh,' sayt he. 'Leave it.'

I took no notice.

Facin the men, I stepped fort and begun stompin and thumpin my feet to the music what were in my skull. As I moved twort em I made low growlin noises in the back of my gullet what soon become great whoops and snarls that were like enough heard by himsen the Prelate and all the souls of Grathico – such were the clamour I made.

I looked back at Withy who seemed none too pleased, glowerin at me as he drew upon his pipe. Throstle pulled the sheet across his mug for the sight were too much for him all agether. The Thrum-Patter were only danced by the womenfolk but I werenoh so poorly at it mysen is what I thought – especial considerin I were dancin upon the dirt and noh a proper floor. As I twirled round and round I could hear the women stompin their feet agin the stone floor of the church. Inside my skull I saw their heavy shoes – worn especial for the dance – what kep time to the Voice of the Prelate, for that were what the dance were for, to give measure and stress to his sermonisin. Claspin the Book in one hand and shakin his cane at the congregation with the other, the Prelate gesticulated wild-like from the pulpit while the women pounded their feet agin the stone – *thrum, patter-patter, thrum, patter-patter, thrum* – keepin time to the cadences of the sermon.

Lord have mercy – thrum patter, patter, thrum

Upon thy soul! – thrum! thrum! thrum!

From the corner of mine eye, I spied the men turn and walk away. Spinnin round I brought the feet agether and ended the Thrum-Patter with a triple thrum, movin fort some as I done it as though it were a war dance forta drive em back to the village. It is mine advisement to allway end a Thrum-Patter on a triple thrum, thatwise souls know ye mean business – that come second in *The Philosophy of the Wastelands*.

Gob open, I smiled some as my breath come hard and fast, mixin with the air and plumin afore me. Eyes glistenin with the cold, I let the venom leave my spirit like it were followin the Closemen, usherin em back from whence they come.

'To Grathico, gowks!' sayt I.

Turnin round, I saw Withy had left me and were walkin his tall and flimsy sen twort the bothy – he were in a distance, still-yet, I could make out my coat draped across his arm. Throstle stood with the sheet tight about the chin, lookin betwix mysen and his long gangly cully. I watched old Spindle-shanks walk away from me, his thin shadow near stretchin back to the sea. I thought him elegant in his way – silent and distant with his gauzy shade cast upon the Wastelands. Mind, I'd ner tell him that, I'd sooner be dead, truth be tolt, so ye'd best keep that to yersen – it will be our wee secret, one beast to another like.

Anywise, I ran some to catch up upon him – Throstle were behind me, near trippin over himsen with the sheet flappin bout the ankles.

'Wait!' sayt he. 'My pegs arenoh as long as yers!'

I calt out to Withy but he didnoh turn round nor acknowledge my hallooin, which I thought were somewhat ill-mannered and unnecessary. He'd get huffy with me on occasions, which amused me some.

'Why ye in such a hurry?' enquizzened I, catchin up to his great towerin sen.

'I'm cold,' sayt he. 'Asides, I were growt tired of yer wee dance, I've noh the stomach to watch ye prancin round makin a show of yersen and all.'

He walked on, starin hard at the ground ahead.

'I come to the Wastes to tell ye of trouble and ye act like a buffoon, puttin us all in peril.'

'Thou hast come cause the Prelate tolt ye.'

'Noh only.'

'Thou hast changed some, Withy, scared thou hast become.'

'For thee.'

41

'For thysen.'

'Both – there is a bad business comin.'

'Hell, so sayeth the Prelate.'

'Aye, and it comes for thee.'

'Let it come,' sayt I, laughin and throwin mysen upon his back.

Withy made a show of protestin – weak mind, as in sooth I donoh think he were all that nettled with me. Anywise, after a spell he resigned himsen to carryin me upon his back and his hand soon appeared over his shoulder – my coat gathered betwix his bony fingers.

'Put it on,' sayt he. 'Ye'll soon be cold after all that exertion.'

There were concern nestled behind the jibin in his voice and I smiled some and did what I were tolt. Settlin down, I rested my skull betwix his shoulder blades as Throstle trotted alongside us. I were too old to be carried on any soul's back, still-yet, there I were starin over Withy's shoulder, the bothy in a distance and the dark sea to the side. It were a fierce handsome view up there, I could even see the spire of the church in Grathico way off in a distance, if I cared to look that is. I lingered on it none though, for it gave me the qualms. The day were cold, still-yet, it were clear – away from mine eyes the sea carried on throwin hersen upon the shore. Relentless so she were, churnin about the wholespell – the fishes must get fierce dizzy tryin to swim about in her squally belly.

Lookin at our slender shades tiltin back twort the sea, it were as though Withy had two heads or I were on great long stilts and Throstle were a malformed wee dog trailin upon the heels. I let my cheek fall agin Withy's back and watched the fierce sparse beauty of the Wastelands jolt up-a-down upon his long lopin strides. I were tired, truth be tolt, and happy to rest my skull and let him carry me home.

42

VI

I were drowsy by the time we reached the bothy, cheek agin Withy's back with the slaver comin from the gob and all. I kep the eyes closed as we stepped across the threshold, Withy bendin his long and gangly sen so as to fit neath the door. Inside, he stooped round the hut afore lowerin me upon the soft and straw things what served as my bed, very tendersome mind for I were gettin the special treatment on account of the fact I were a much maligned and troubled soul – *There, there, starvelin of the Wastes, rest thy poor irregular skull.*

Hearin their footsteps move over to the window, I snortled some and pretended to go to the land of sloom, true and proper.

'Did he say aught about comin back?'
'Sayt he'll noh come – I'll try again.'
'Then we go?'
Naught.

43

'Withy?'

'Aye, then we go.'

'He looks poorly,' whispered Throstle. 'Is it eatin the curdle and fishes from the sea what done that to him?'

'I donoh know.'

'They are feedin on his insides.'

'What?'

'The fishes.'

'Quiet, Throstle.'

'Praps it is the sprites and imps of the Wastes what have hollowed his flesh?'

Throstle become silent, vain-waitin for Withy to say somethin.

'His eyes have changed. Hast thou seen orbs as fierce and cold and bright as that? A spirit stares out from inside that skull, somethin noh of this world.'

Peakin some, I saw Withy were sittin by the window, starin across the Wastelands.

'Ye are only quiet when ye agree.'

Still he sayt naught.

'We shouldnoh be here,' sayt Throstle.

'We see him home, we do that for him.'

'Home? This? Thou art noh here to see him home. We shall perish in the Wastes!'

'Quiet, Throstle, he isnoh asleep.'

Throstle spun round to stare upon me layin prone upon the bed.

'Art thou?' sayt Withy.

Openin the orbs, I propped the skull upon the palm – very puckish-like.

'*Spirits of the Wastes ner sleep nor sloom,*' crooned I. 'Does thou noh mind the songs of thy weantime, Throstle?'

44

'I didnoh mean . . .'

'Whisht, it doesnoh matter, and ye Withy should know better, for the Wastes is a wild and precarious place without sentiment and is no soul's home.'

He turnt to me with a very weary look.

'That come next in *The Philosophy of the Wastelands*,' I tolt him.

'The philosophy of what?' enquizzened he with the mug all squishy.

'Ner ye mind.'

It were true what I tolt him a course, even though somespells I had come to consider this barren stretch of bog and rock my home it werenoh and ner could be, for noh even I could live for allway in limbo. The Wastes is only where I reside for the moment, so a spake, should ye wants to write me a letter or the like:

> *Dear Beast-boy,*
> *I hear it is fierce cold and desolate roamin the Wastes all*
> *by yer lonesome – poor thing. I have knitted ye a jumper forta*
> *keep yer bones warm.*
> *Yers verily,*
> *Beast-girl xx*

Ye may send it to me at the followin address: *Beast-boy, The Old Abandoned Bothy, The Wastelands, care of the spirits what languish there.* Put it in a bottle or write it in yer skull – burn it if ye like, for it'll reach me, sure and certain.

Anywise, Withy stayed by the window starin across the Wastelands like he were expectin somethin to appear upon the horizon. Throstle wouldnoh keep still but paced round the hut with the orbs wide and jittery, noh touchin anythin for fear it might infect him.

'Move thy gangly pegs, Withy,' sayt I, kickin the lollopin limbs what were sprawled halfway across the bothy.

He grunted some and pulled the legs in.

'Hungry?' enquizzened I, motionin twort the cured fishes what hung from the rafters.

Withy shook the skull and pretended noh to notice Throstle givin him daggers with the orbs.

'We cannoh eat that, well thou knows,' sayt he, unturnin from the window.

'Then ye will go hungry.'

'We have brought our own,' sayt Throstle.

'Those squalid roisterous birds what fill the sky, no doubt.'

'Aye, what else?'

The gulls and fowl were the main fare of the village for it were sayt that cause they roamed the skies they was closer to the Holy Wraith and were therefore proper food for the God-fearin and devout. It seemed forgotted that most birds of the Quag fed upon fishes they plucked from the seas with their very own gobs. Most of the birds upon the island spent half the day dippin in and out of that sinful sliver of salt and water eatin the very creatures spurned by the righteous souls of Grathico.

Reachin aneath the sheet into his coat, Throstle pulled out a package wrapped in cloth. Placin it on the rickety table he begun to unfold it, which caused me to reel some for it contained the familiar stench of the village. Grathico for allway reeked of the rottin carcasses of the untolt fowl what were kilt and eaten each year – the stench waftin from the piles of discarded bones afore they was crushed and scattered upon the fields. The burden of catchin the birds was borne by the Fowlers, a guild of men skilled in the art of catchin fowl whose duty

46

it were to provide the village with sustenance. The Fowlers used a number of methods to entrap the birds, inclusive of gins and such, but the most common were with the fowlin rods – long poles made from coppiced hazel or birch with loops of horse hair at the end. Ropes reinforced in goat hide to prevent their snappin agin the rocks were tethered to great metal pegs what were driven into the earth. The other end were tied round the girth of the Fowler who would then scale down the cliff back-wise. These men had a knack for negotiatin the cliffs and were second only to the goats of all God's creatures in climbin rocky and inaccessible scarps – part goat emsens it were sayt among Grathicans. The birds were rendered easy prey on account of the instinct to raise their young, for such was their interest in propagatin their own species that they chose to die upon the egg rather-an escape with their lives. They'd squawk and holler as the men approached but remained steadfast till the horse hair were drawn tight round their gullets and they were snatched from their rocky crags, nests raided for eggs.

We calt em gulls or fowl in general but the Quag were swamped by birds of all kinds; gairfowl, cormorants, gan-nets, kittiwakes, puffins, great skuas, guillemots, petrels and the black and white auks, or razorbills as they were otherwise knowt. Cliffwise were the most successful means of catchin fowl but it were also the most perilous and there were a soul or two most years who lost his life to the unforgivin rocks or to Melas' dark and secretive sen. The Fowlers were revered for the peril of their trade and the life it brought to the village.

As weans we played Skull and Feathers upon a stone slab riven into squares. Each contender had a bird skull and the idea were to roll the dice and move it so as to collect as many of the other wean's feathers as possible; whosoever won could choose to keep or crush his opponent's skull – bird skull that is a course. If ye were crushed three times ye were out the tussle all agether till the next round begun, which could be a good longspell, dependin. The feathers become like currency with what ye could swap and trade and buy things, so a wean what bin crushed out the tussle were a poor and forlorn creature much derided by the others. Skull and Feathers were a serious business among the whelps and I saw more-an a few scuffles break out – hands clawin at each other while shrill voices cursed the heavens. The geese they kep for allway at their sides honked and threshed the wings about as they scattered down the narrows while their wee wardens rolled in the dirt, fingers wrapped round each other's gullets.

'*Keep or crush! Keep or crush!*' chanted the others as they watched on.

Anywise, while Throstle parcelled out the fowl meat betwix himsen and Withy, I begun fixin a meal of sorts from wispy thing-o-ma-gigs and blewits and wee bits of broiled sea curdle. Slingin it upon the old cracked plate, I untied the last of the cured fishes strung from the ceilin. Withy shovelled his dinner from his hand as Throstle kep his eyes upon me, his face growin squishy and horrified as I begun to eat.

'Dost thou want none then?'

Walkin across the hut I helt the plate under his nose, whereupon he begun retchin and splutterin like a mooncalf. It were as I were pushin the fish under Throstle's naysayin skull that the bothy become lit up by a flash of lightnin and we three turnt to look upon the window.

'Tolt ye,' sayt Withy, helpin himsen to another gobful of gull.

Thunder come next as we pressed our mugs agin the glass. There werenoh as yet a single show of rain but hoverin over the horizon, black and grey clouds swirled and folded in on each other. Huddled agin the window we watched the dark chimeras – startled waxen by sheet lightnin – loom distant in a sky displeased with all creation.

'Ye knowt it were comin!' bawled Throstle.

Withy turnt the skull from him.

'Ye did this on purpose!'

'Aye, Throstle,' sayt he. 'I commanded the heavens to part in order to vex ye.'

'Ye knowt it were comin and sayt naught.'

'Thou hast allway sayt mine augurin were vain incantation and witchery.'

'What do we do?'

'Wait it out.'

'Here?'

'Is there a choice?'

It were sayt that at the end of each lightnin bolt there sizzled the soul of a sinner or evil spirit what God had stricken from the earth. It were for this reason Grathicans were unbidden to be outdoors when His almighty vengeance were in the sky. God-fearin souls were to stay indoors with the skulls bowed and pray for mercy. It were agin Grathican law and considered vanity and insolence most grave to raise thy profane mug to His inviolable wrath.

Throstle wrung his hands afore marchin himsen straight to the corner of the bothy; kneelin down he faced the wall and begun prayin. Withy and I huddled agin the window, listenin to divine commination rumblin in the skies above – in silence we gawked upon the storm's black and menacin sen marchin upon the Quag as we munched quiet-like on the flesh what sustained us.

The winds picked up in a sudden, rattlin the old dilapidated bones of the bothy as lightnin scolded evil spirts out to sea. The closer it come the more fidgety and restless Throstle were – switchin betwix prayin and pacin up-a-down the hut, he helt the vial of consecrated ground in his hand, pressin it agin his lips and passin it across his body in the sign of the cross. Withy sat in his corner smokin and lookin out the window – orbs wide, he stared into the dusk like he were prayin or willin the storm ado its worse.

'I donoh feel safe here. No! I donoh feel safe!' bawled Throstle, stoppin his pacin long enough to tremble and stammer. 'The roof shall cave in and we shall be crushed!' sayt he.

Throstle were prone to exaggeration. Natheless, watchin the roof quiver and quave, I thought he had a point.

'We could take shelter in the cave up beyond, where I store firewood,' sayt I.

'We should leave!'

'We are noh spose to be outside, hast thou forgotted?' sayt Withy.

'We will soon be outside anywise if we stay here!'

'I think he's right,' sayt I.

'Course I'm right!'

Sighin, Withy hauled himsen from the chair with great effort.

'Right so, shall we go then?'

We clustered the blankets, spears and food afore leavin. The wind was such that I had to put all my weight agin the door forta open it – slammin shut behind us, it near come off its hinges. Outside, the weather jostled and harried us about. Throstle stayed close, leppin and jumpin round like the ground were hot coals. Turnin to check on Withy, my hair whipped about my skull like wee vicious tongues, lickin and stingin the orbs. His long and lean sen were laggin behind, hunched agin the weather. Above him the sky were wild; a bright full moon peeked its skull out every-now-a-then from inbetwix the sinistrous doomy clouds what blew quick-like across the night. Withy stopped and turnt to face the storm; skull raised to the heavens he helt out his arms forta test the strength of the wind. Standin in the wet, he looked like a defiant wintry tree sprung from the barren soil of the Wastelands – forlorn and fruitless, branches raised to a savage and un- yieldin sky.

The smell of static and insurrection were in the air as the welkin swelled and swirled divergin colours – a sickly yellow inbetwix. Things become fraught and uneasy as the violence stewed above. It were excitin some, truth be tolt, like the dark clouds were munchin on emsens, chewin on their own angry flesh – like the sky were devourin itsen.

'There it is,' sayt I.

Throstle stopped and swivelled the skull about.

'Where?!'

I raised the arm and pointed to a dark patch in the jagged jut of rock up a ways a bit.

'Where?!' sayt he.

The poor frightened lump were near aside himsen with the nerves till a flash of lightnin lit up the whole rock face and put him out of his misery.

'There it is! I saw it!'

He took off then, desperate as he were to save himsen from the weather. When I caught him up he were attemptin to scramble up the talus clustered at the base of the cliff – one hand clasped tight round the sheet while his squat limbs slid up-a-down in a flurry. I gave his rump a heave and off he went, shootin up the rocks into the cave without so much as glancin back. Inside, I found him nestled in a dark nook afore I turnt to watch Withy clamberin up the scree. Soon as he entered he wrapped his long lanky sen in the blanket I throwt him and stood, all shivery and wet, watchin the tetchy rankled night bloomin grey and black.

'Looks like hersen the sea – cep in the sky,' sayt he, bringin the blanket tight round the shoulders.

'Aye.'

'The world bin turnt upsy-down.'

'Allway sayt I would,' sayt I, lookin at him slantwise with a smirk, but he were quiet and thoughtful, so the two of us just stood there a spell watchin the mysterious battle bein waged in the welkin.

'Ye will noh come back?' sayt he.

'Ye think the Prelate will welcome me back into the fold, open his arms forta embrace me? Thou knows how it is, Withy – there is no goin back.'

I left him at the mouth of the cave and retreated further into the dark to bed down for the night. What with the noise and the cold there werenoh much sloom to be had and I flittered betwix wakin and sleepin. We were well into the night when the howl of wind and crash of thunder wakened me. Openin the eyes a tittle I saw Withy pacin back-a-fort on the further side of the cave. Throstle ducked the head and pretended to be asleep when I turnt to look upon him. Openin the orbs proper, I become alert to a strange current circulatin round the dark and cold of the cave.

'Why does thou noh rest some, Withy?'

He near lep out the skin when I sayt that – turnin, he stared upon me with the eyes gleamin out the black hole of his skull.

It were unnervin, truth be tolt, there were somethin wild and confused in his big tormented orbs.

'Sleep upon it,' sayt I, 'colours are clearer in the morn.'

The storm lit up the cave, alightin three stranded souls in the dark. Spinnin round, Withy slid his back down the rock and buried his mug in his hands.

It were half-light when next I wakened, both Withy and Throstle was still asleep, so I wrapped the blanket round the shoulders and shuffled to the mouth of the cave. The sun were peepin its skull over the Quag and weavin its first greedy fingers through the Wastes. Coverin mine eyes, I stepped into the light and felt a shiver work its way through the limbs as the warmth seeped into my bones. It were perfect out, like the storm had ner happened or had brought a great cleansin to the sky and our godforsaken ait. Standin there, baskin in the splendour of the mornin and all that flap, I felt the ground aneath me shift. I thought I heard somethin in a distance too, like a quantity of water surgin fort then drainin away. The jolt were such that I stepped fort some so as to check my balance. Withy and Throstle were still sound asleep for it hadnoh bin enough to waken their sloomy skulls.

Takin up the spear, I squelched seaward through the Wastes what had become fierce fenny from the night afore. I were hummin to mysen, very insouciant and the like, conjurin all kinds of blether in the skull till I come to the edge of the cliff, near where Withy and I bin the day afore. Stoppin dead in my tracks, the blanket fell away from my shoulders and I stood in the cold mornin air – the Quag become still and I heard naught, cep the sound of the sea and mine own breath heavin in and out my chest as I gawped at the creature what lay large and wilderin upon our shore.

VII

She were grey-black and glistenin in the sun. A wave broke upon the shore and rushed twort her – liftin her powerful tail she lashed at the water what turnt and crawled away like a scolded pup. Judgin by the long trench her body'd carved in the sand she'd come ashore with great force. I watched the water smoothin out and erodin the trough she'd made but she could just as easy have come from the sky were how I felt. I could just as easy imagine her plummetin through the clouds as ploughin through the sea – she werenoh of this world, that were for sure and certain. Mine innards felt like they was tryin to leap out my skin and rush twort her. She were vast and monstrous and awe-makin and my heart beat hard agin my chest as the sea kep comin for her – lappin at her tail afore retreatin again, tryin to coax her back into the depths.

I'd ner thought anythin frightenin nor beautiful afore, noh like her. I find it blush-makin to say, but she felt like truth to me, a single great truth lyin big and grey upon the sand. A gift bin brought me were what I thought, she were the thing I'd bin longin for without knowin I'd bin longin for it. A creature from another world had collided with ours – a reckonin she might properwise be knowt, a great reckonin had washed upon our shores, and I ran twort it.

Keepin the eyes upon her the whole way down I near tripped over mine own limbs afore leppin off the rocks and landin in the sand. As I approached, I pulled up some, for the small black eye on the side of her skull were trackin me. I musta appeared a sight to her in the ragamuffin get-up with the face pale as a ghost and eyes glistenin from the wind – mine awestruck gob were wide open like a dozy mooncalf and all.

'Howthee?' sayt I, quiet-like.

She answered me none a course but instead thudded her immense tail into the sand which I felt pass good and proper through the bones. It frightened me some, that were for sure and certain, and I dared go no closer. After a while though, I figured she werenoh angry with me as such but more frustrated at her own predicament. She let out a long mournful cry and I took that as my cue to approach her.

Aside me she were a mountain of flesh – a soul couldnoh appreciate her standin atop the cliff. I'd no idea what largeness a creature such as her were spose to grow but she seemed a monstrous size – just standin next her gave me a dizziness in the skull. She were towerin and grey, and things growt from her – barnacles and the like. Her whole body seemed to be drippin with brine, like it were comin from her skin, like she were sweatin the sea from her pores.

'What's thou doin here?' enquizzened I, which were a scatter-brained thing to enquizzen, sure and certain, but what's a soul spose to say to a beast such as her?

I rested my hand upon her, just behind the mouth, then moved down her body some. I felt her small black eye strainin itsen to view me – *Who is this beast-boy, in the silly clothes, runnin his grubby hands all over me?* Her skin were tough like armour and werenoh like skin at all. She had scars upon it, great long gouges what ran down her sides from her battles in the sea, fightin the creatures what lurk within and the boats of man what had the cheek to pass through her realm. It looked like an ancient language bin carved into her flesh – runnin my fingers over the ruts and whorls of her wounds I read the mysteries of the deep like a blind man what comprehends with his fingers.

In the muzzy fluff betwix mine ears I conjured images of her battles – saltwater and blood mixin like the Devil's tincture in the darkest depths of the sea. I heard the sounds and felt the blows of the savage clashes what took place far away from the eyes of man. I imagined a narwhal, skin the colour of death, drivin its twisted knarry tusk down her side; soundin her rage through the sea the Leviathan kep the small black stone of her eye starin into the dark expanse as she battered the narwhal's skull with a swipe of her tail – whereupon the unfortunate creature become still and lifeless, sinkin into the depths of Melas' murky womb.

'Thous bin in a few scraps,' sayt I.

She kep quiet, eyeballin me suspicious-like.

'Bin in one or two mysen,' I tolt her. 'Though I cannoh crush the boats of men with naught but my skull, and I'm the king of no realm – cep the Wastelands a course, but thou canst have it if thou likes.'

Thanks very much beast-boy, sayt she, *that is most generous of ye and all, but, truth be, it is already mine – allway has bin, allway will be. Still and all, thank ye very much, thou hast warmed my big cold heart.* That is what the Leviathan sayt to me, paraphrased some a course, but that, more or less, were the gist of what she sayt.

I kep my hands upon her, imaginin her scraps in the sea. I imagined her rammin her skull into the middle of a ship and snappin it in two. I cheered her on, willin her to victory in her battles agin man. I saw over and over how the planks of the ship's hull crumbled like twigs afore her great mass, the men aboard screamin and cryin – makin an unholy show of emsens and all. Ner again would they see their kinfolk, for the Leviathan had deemed otherwise – she'd decided it were their destiny to become salt and seasonin for the great dark soup what is the sea. Amen.

I worked my way round her, givin her tail a wide berth for I didnoh fancy bein caught aneath that great angry limb. Her eye, tiny in her vast skull, were trackin me the wholespell – pickin me up as I come back alongside her. It were like she were lookin straight through this world into the next or praps she were blind somewise and saw nothin at all, if that make any nous. Her stare made a big gapin hole in my gizzards, still-yet, I thought I understood it – there were somethin in the muzzy glaze of that eye what were familiar.

She walloped the tail into the sand aside me for I'd come too close and she were lettin me know.

'Ye can stop with the tail,' I tolt her, 'I know yer there and all.'

She moaned and beat her tail even harder agin the shore – *I'll thud the tail if I like, beast-boy, I shall do whatsoever I like with the goddamn tail.*

Cannoh argue with that, can ye?

I begun talkin to her some, tryin to calm her, tellin her it would be alright and all. I donoh think I were in my right mind, truth be tolt. I enquizzened her about how she got here and why she'd come. I tolt her she were in parts unfamiliar to her. I tolt her to watch out for the Prelate for he were a devious soul, the like of which I doubt could even be found in the innermost gloom of Melas' dank and fathomless depths. I tolt her I'd look after her, for while she were a fierce and awe-makin beast, I knowt she were helpless out the water. I knowt she musta felt naked and heavy without Melas round her – without the support of the sea, the weight of her own flesh musta felt like it were near crushin her.

In a sudden it come to me that she were fierce thirsty for the dark and salty brine. I cursed mysen for all the blather-spake and ran to the water's edge. Crouchin down I made my hands into a bowl and waited for Melas to come to me. By the time I reached Levi though, the tiny wrigglin sea what were trapped betwix my fingers had well-nigh disappeared and I throwt what were left over her. The sea upon her flesh seemed to put her in a frenzy, she moaned some and begun thrashin her tail about as though she were in great longin for its cool and watery sen, as though she had a thirst for it all over her body. She begun thumpin her tail over and over like it were a song, like it were a code or message or somethin – she were impressin her longin and distress into the sand were what I thought. I turnt and ran back to the sea but the water I could bring her were pitiful and near gone each spell I reached her. I needed things what would carry and keep the sea upon her. I tolt Levi my plan, throwt a bit of water on her best I could and took off in the direction of the bothy.

When I arrived, Withy and Throstle were approachin up the way a bit. They was returnin from the cave, marchin brisk-like and agitated. Throstle were stumblin through the Waste-

lands, the blessed sheet still wrapped around him as he wiped
sloom from his eyes and swivelled the skull this-way-a-that in
case any imps or devils were sneakin upon him. Withy himsen were singin forta ward off the spirits.

I were on my haunches, winnowin through the dross inside
the bothy when his tall and spindly shade darkened my door.

'Mornin,' sayt he, very haughty and put out.

I kep searchin for the blankets and do-gacks I were lookin
for.

'Mornin,' sayt he, somewhat louder.

'Heard the first spell, Withy.'

'Ye should answer the first spell then. Fine show leavin us
in the cave – we'll be headin back to Grathico, we've put oursens in peril for naught.'

I turnt round and found him blockin the door so as Throstle couldnoh enter, for his round and frightened sen didnoh
want to be out in the Wastes any longer-an he had to.

'Where the rest of the blankets and buckets?' sayt I to
mysen.

Throstle tried to nudge his way through a gap but Withy
tightened his grip on the door frame and adjusted his bony
rump so as to prevent it.

'What has ye so nettled?' enquizzened he, studyin my mug.

'She has come ashore,' sayt I, short of breath.

'Who?'

'The beast.'

'What?'

'The Leviathan.'

Throstle stopped tryin to get past Withy and poked his
head round the long limbs forta gawk upon me.

'Ye spake in tongues.'

59

'Her great sen what live in the sea – the one ye sayt bin cirlin the Quag, she has come ashore.'

'What's thou mean, she has come ashore?'

'She is upon the sand, aneath the cliff, where we was yestermorn.'

Withy were quiet a spell.

'Thou art in earnest?'

'Aye.'

'What the blankets and buckets for?'

'To keep her wet – she is drownin.'

'Drownin? A beast what lives in the sea is drownin?'

'I mean, she is the opposite of drownin, ye know, on land.'

'I think ye have the fever.'

Turnin from him in irritation, I clustered the blankets and whatnoh best I could and pushed past his stubborn, gangly sen.

'Where ye off to then?' enquizzened he.

When I didnoh respond he left the door and come after me. Throstle remained at the threshold of the bothy what were now without obstacle. Torn betwix stayin on his ownsome or followin, he turnt and scuttled after us.

VIII

'Tolt ye,' sayt I.

Withy stood atop the cliff, spear in hand, gawkin at hersen below.

'Come on!' bawled I, grabbin hold of his shirt but he would-noh move so I took off without him.

Runnin across the sand, I rested my hand upon her.

'Sayt I'd be back didnoh I?'

Levi looked at me dubious-like.

'I've come to put the sea back on thy flesh and all.'

I dropped the blankets and things and ran two buckets down to Melas. On my way back I saw old Spindle-shanks takin his own fair time to reach us. With my hands full and the sea spillin over the rims of the buckets I motioned with the skull for him to hurry himsen, but he were payin me no heed and had his eyes fixed on the beast what lay upon our shore. Throstle were halfway up the cliff, comin down backwise like a child with the wee stumpy pegs searchin all nervous and jittery for a spot to rest emsens. I let out a weary sigh, thinkin it woulda bin best if they'd both gone back to Grathico.

I throwt one of the buckets upon Levi's back but it seemed to wet her little on account of her bein so vast and all. The second bucket I poured slowise across her skull while she watched me close with the orb. Rubbin the saltwater into her flesh, I tolt her it'd be alright.

'Make yersen useful Withy and soak those blankets in the sea.'

He turnt to me.

'Hurry thysen!'

'But the water . . .'

'It willnoh harm ye!'

Still he didnoh move but gawked upon the whale. Throstle come bustlin up next – stoppin a good distance away he refused to come closer.

'Will ye come help, Throstle!'

'It is monstrous!' sayt he.

'It is no such thing!'

'It is the Beast!'

'Blather-spake!'

Turnin to me with wide, panic-stricken orbs, Throstle clasped his wee hands agether.

'*In that day the Lord with his sore and great and strong sword shall punish Leviathan the piercin serpent, that crooked serpent and he shall slay the dragon what is in the sea.*'

I looked hard at his round and tremblin sen squirmin upon the sand.

'*And in that day sing ye unto her a vineyard of red wine,*' sayt I, finishin his wee quote from the Book.

'What is it if noh the Devil?'

I looked at her vast sen stretched upon the shore.

'I donoh know.'

Throstle begun steppin backwise.

'Come here!'

'I willnoh touch it!'

'Ye willnoh have to – take the buckets and fill em with water,' sayt I, pickin one up and holdin it out to him.

He looked to Withy, but his long gangly sen were still possessed by the whale, under her spell, so he were. Slowise, Throstle begun to approach – losin patience I made a stern face and shook the bucket what were in my hand. Quicksteppin twort me, he thrust out his stubby arm just enough forta reach it.

'Put the bucket down, Throstle,' sayt Withy. 'We will noh be waterin any beasts.'

Throstle looked betwix himsen and mysen and slowise he lowered the bucket to the sand. As he were rightin himsen, Levi thrashed her tail agin the shore. Throstle near lost his life and disappeared behind Withy, who himsen had moved back some with the fright.

'Whisht, Levi,' sayt I, walkin over to stroke her flank.

'Levi?'

'Her name.'

'She tolt ye hersen, I spose.'

'Praps she did,' sayt I, fixin Withy with fierce menacin orbs. 'Praps she did tell me.'

He shook the skull, despair and unbelief itsen.

'It is as the Prelate says, ye in the Wastes, besotted and fawnin over a creature that Melas hersen has cast out. We can be no part of this, thou knows. This is the Devil's work – it is unnatural.'

'Grathico seems natural to ye does it, Withy? Praps it is the preachin and the torture what seems most splendid and natural to ye?'

'God's compassion is vigilant and unmerciful.'

'What does that mean? Dost thou even know? Thou sounds like him and all.'

I turnt forta cluster the blankets – concentratin the orbs on her large grey sen.

'Best ye two go back to Grathico. Report to the Prelate on the Wastes and the mudlark ye found lurkin there . . .'

Turnin the skull, I saw Withy had unfettered the spear from his back while Throstle had become pale as the sheet wrapped round him. I looked betwix the two of em with a very curious expression upon the mug.

'What's this then?'

Withy buried his skull, very sheepish-like.

'What was thou conspirin ado behind my back?'

'Naught, brother.'

'Brother now is it?'

Silence.

'What's the spear for?'

Withy looked at the spear as though it had alighted upon his hand by magic, as though some sorcery of the Wastelands put it there.

'I wouldnoh . . . ner would,' sayt he, stammerin as though his tongue had become very thick and clumsy in a sudden.

'Ye would ner, still-yet, the spear just happened upon thy hand, did it? Where was ye plannin to lance me, betwix the shoulders? Wast thou concentrated on the space bewtix my shoulder blades?!'

He shook the skull, forlorn and hangdog.

64

'The Prelate were sendin souls forta end ye, if I could bring ye back were the only way.'

'So that the very same could happen in Grathico? Were this what all the pacin last night were about?'

'I knowt ye would ner return,' sayt he, lowerin the eyes. 'I thought it best if it come from me and noh his gowks.'

'That is a most profound sentiment, Withy. Thou art an heroic and noble specimen, sure and certain. Souls with yer depth of character are few and far betwix upon this ait.'

He become all shamefaced and flathered.

'I'll turn the back,' sayt I, 'praps thy courage will return.'

I did as I sayt and turnt the back upon em, standin with the arms outstretched and all.

'For what dost thou wait?' enquizzened I, turnin the skull over the shoulder. 'Brother.'

It seemed a longspell afore the spear were pitched into the sand, noh far from my feet. I blanched some, for I'd the orbs squeezed shut, braced for the seerin pain of the spear to pass through me. When I turnt round he were already walkin up the sand twort the cliff.

'Say naught about the Leviathan!' bawled I.

He turnt to face me.

'How long does thou think it can be kep a secret?!'

'Keep thy gob shut.'

'Havenoh I allway?'

Throstle looked betwix Withy and I with the ears pricked, very attentive and all he were.

'I'll say naught but it will only delay what will come,' sayt he, turnin the back upon me.

Throstle had bin slitherin away the wholespell, keepin an orb upon me and the whale as he retreated.

'Say naught about the Leviathan, Throstle.'

He become still at the sound of my voice.

'Or I'll come visit ye in Grathico.'

Lookin past me, he stared upon the whale with fear and awe.

'She and I both will come down upon thee if aught is sayt.'

He nodded the skull very meek and trotted off after Withy.

Turnin back to Levi I tolt her noh to mind those spine-less gowks and took up the blankets forta march down to Melas. Comin back I spied the two of em standin atop the cliff lookin down upon me. Withy opened the gob and started singin the 'Mortal Song' what is sung when a soul has died; he sung it in the village forta announce a death or while marchin afore a funeral procession alongside the Wailin Women what clutched at their bosoms as the dark weepin veils swirled about their skulls. Anywise, there he stood atop the cliff, singin the 'Mortal Song' to me in the Wastelands – foretellin things to come, I expect.

What wonderous love be this, O my soul, O my soul!
What wonderous love be this, O my soul!
What wonderous love be this,
What caused the Lord of bliss,
To bear the dreadful curse,
O my soul, O my soul,
To bear the dreadful curse, O my soul.
To God and to the lamb, I will sing, I will sing!
To God and to the lamb, I will sing!
And when from death I'm free, I'll sing and joyful be,
And through all eternity, I'll sing on, I'll sing on,
Throughout eternity, I'll sing on.

Throstle turnt and begun walkin into the Wastes, leavin Withy to sing by his lonesome.

To bear the dreadful curse,
O my soul, O my soul . . .

It werenoh long afore a short and stubby arm reappeared forta tug on Withy's waist and, reluctant-like, he moved off – the two disappearin behind the black rock, Withy's voice waftin back to me through the Wastelands.

To bear the dreadful curse, O my soul . . .

IX

I were glad to be on mine ownsome with Levi and had taken
to caressin and pamperin her which she seemed to tolerate
on account of the fact I were bringin the sea to her. I were still
agitated bout Withy and Throstle as I paced to-a-fro throwin
the water upon her. I were wound up, sure and certain, gesticulatin with the hands and so fort.

'This is what it is like,' muttered I, 'this is what ye have to
put up with.'

As I fussed over her, I tolt her all about the village and the
treachery of the souls what lived there. I tolt her my whole sorry
story, so a spake – *They did this, Levi, and then they did that!
And now I'm in the Wastes all on my lonesome.* Levi thumped
her limb agin the shore – *That's what I'd do, beast-boy, if it were
up to me, I'd crush em aneath the tail so as they'd ner bother ye
again and then ye and me could take to the seas – spend the rest
our days slippin through Melas' dark and glistenin gizzards.*

That's what I thought she were sayin anywise, though she were mute for the most part, followin me with the wee black eye. The gibberish what spilt from my gob and her silence were only what were bein sayt, or unsayt, on the surface. A whole nother conversation, for which there was no words, were takin place alongside it – aneath it, so a spake. Truth be tolt, it were the kind of conversation what can only be understood by beast-boys and fierce wild creatures from the deep what have, in recent spells, bin washed upon a shore. It is a peculiar and strange language what I couldnoh teach ye even if I wanted – which I donoh. She were transmittin things to me somewise, through her skull praps, for I believe that is how they communicate among their own sens in the sea, like they've ears inside their skulls what receive the songs of their kinfolk and creatures of their own kind – beast-boys, for example. Thinkin hard upon it, it make nous havin their ears inside their skulls on account of the fact that if they were on the outside they would just fill and slosh with water and they'd noh hear aught. I consider such explications helpful, for ye will noh know about these things unless ye are in regular conversations with immense and mysterious creatures from the sea – which is doubtful, truth be tolt. Anywise, howsoever she were sayin it, it were received straight into mine innards what were become all jittery and tangled.

I put Grathico and all its gowks out the skull and concentrated good and proper on tendin to Levi. Feelin her aneath the fingers were a calmin and ruminative thing. I rubbed the water into her wounds like it were an ointment what might soothe and heal her. She seemed to like it well enough, for she made low croonin sounds way in back of her throat and down her belly as she flapped the tail about, soft and lackadaisy agin the sand – *That's noh half bad*, sayt she, *ye are some use after all*.

It werenoh easy tryin to get the sodden blankets over her, for they was small for her immense size and only covered her vast body in patches. I throwt em over her length and kep pourin water on em to keep em fresh. I worked away like that for a good longspell, though in the end I were still noh satisfied and so went back to the bothy forta collect the twine and knife and to bring spears and some of the wood what were kep stored in the cave – I wouldnoh leave her a course, and planned to spend the night camped next her upon the shore. I took the blankets off her one by one and sat down forta make holes round their edges while she hersen looked on – *Thou art a rare and curious beast-child, sure and certain*. Through the holes I bound the blankets agether with twine – it werenoh the most skillful of work but it done the job all the same. I sewed two or three agether at a time and slung em over her like a rope, then I had to spread em across her spine and flanks. Once I were done I stood back and looked at her covered with the blankets and, truth be tolt, they suited her I reckoned. They looked like some kind of armour upon her, what with the crude stitchin and the mottled grey-green colour of the cloth and all. I werenoh sure what she made of em hersen but they seemed to nettle her none – the swishin of the tail stopped, more or less, and she werenoh moanin neither, but just followin me very curious with the eye.

As the sun started to set I built a fire, pilin the wood away from her so as noh to dry her skin. I kep prattlin away all the while – blather-spake for the most part. I tolt her bout the yawl I'd hid within the hollow of the cliff and how I could sail the seas with her thatwise, I tolt her we could catch fishes agether and pursue other

70

such seafarin ventures. Anywise, after the fire were lit I kep at her with the water, makin sure the blankets stayed sodden, adjustin em some so as to cover as much of her as I could. Every-now-a-then I'd to run back to the fire forta stop the shiverin and make sure it stayed lit and burnin. It were delicious some, warmin the bones and dryin the feet – I took the boots off and left em right up close, warmin the leather by the flames so as they near burnt the toes off when I put em on again. Then I'd just sit with a blanket wrapped round me watchin Levi while wisps of burnin wood lep from the fire like smoulderin insects shaken from a nest. I kenned Levi were watchin me too for I could see the fire reflected in her eye – a flickerin orange shape dancin right there in the centre of that wee black stone.

I become tired after a spell, runnin hither-thither to tend her, so I curled mysen round the fire forta watch her from that laid-down sideward position and listen to the fire sizzle and crack as it feasted upon the wood. I could still hear the sea, though she musta bin fierce tired as well for she were no longer bitin down agin the sand but collapsin upon it. Quiet-like, the dark brine fell upon the shore sighin and slushin about as though she were susurratin to all the Quag, tellin it to hush some – *Shhhh*, sayt she, *the Leviathan is come*.

I felt the thud of Levi's tail rise through the sand. She were makin low keenin sounds every-now-a-then and I sat up forta look upon her but she were allway just lyin there. With the dim-lustred light of the moon glistenin upon her she looked like an island hersen, a great dark mass risin from the water what glimmered behind her. Mine orbs begun to shut of their own accord but I kep forcin em open as I were afeared somethin may happen to her, like praps she may wriggle her vast sen backwise into the sea – though that seemed a fabled and

71

impossible thing even to mysen. Breath exploded out the top of her skull and made me blanch with the fright, the fine mist of sea what come with it fell all feathery-like upon the shore, glitterin some in the glaze of the moon.

Anywise, that were how I spent the first cold night with the Leviathan. After what seemed an endless longspell the sun peeped its guilty head over the top of the sea – *Ah, sorry there, lads but would ye mind if I like, rose and all, terrible sorry, but it's about time another day begun upon yer wretched and gloomy ait.* Warmin the earth, it begun suckin the wet from the sand, so I clustered all the blankets from round the fire and lay next to Levi. It were strange some, snugglin up agin her flank, I werenoh afeared she'd roll atop me or anythin – truth be, it were comfortin to feel her great and mysterious mass behind me.

Last thing I mind were her moanin and mewlin and whatnoh – mine orbs become shut good and proper and I fell asleep to the waul of the whale, which is heard by few, truth be tolt. The keenin of the Leviathan is a song to the Wastelands from the belly of the sea – it is a cradle song, more or less – a lament for all those things what have no name and drift through the world unclaimed.

Ye should write that in yer wee book of philosophy, Levi tolt me as I were noddin off.

'Aye,' sayt I, stretchin the gob in a gapin yawn. 'I'll do just that in the morn.'

Do it now, sayt she, *otherwise sloom will steal it from ye and ye'll forget in the night.*

But it were late for that, for I were already asleep, plus it werenoh quite right for *The Philosophy of the Wastelands*, somewise it were too slippery to be captured in words, asides which, some things should be lost in the night and dissolved in sloom – noh everythin needs be catalogued is what I reckon.

72

X

'Ye sleep with the Beastht!'
It were the shrill and nettlesome voice of a child what wakened me. Somethin were bein throwt upon me, shell or stone, whatsoever it were landed with a thud afore rollin some in the sand.

'Ye lie with the Devil!'

Another oddment bounced across the shore and rolled into my gut. I tried openin the eyes but the sun were fierce strong and they took time adjustin emsens. In a distance, hazy with light, were the Stone Thrower lookin like a sulky wee angel come forta visit me. He were wide-orbed and pale, blinkin at me like an owl and clutchin his poke of stones as though – even at a distance, while I were horizontalwise and all – I might still be fixin to snatch em from him. Heavy with sloom, I raised mysen and – with an outstretched arm – begun movin twort him. The boy secured the flap over his poke and took a few steps backwise.

'I were tolt to inform ye that if I werenoh allowed pathage or if any harm were to come to me, the Prelate would visit all hith wrath upon ye!'

I raised my hand forta block the sun and to suggest to the child he may hush some, for I werenoh long wakened and nay in the mood for all his shoutin and carry-on.

'That's why ye were out this far the other day,' sayt I. 'Prelate tolt ye of her presence in the sea and bade ye come deeper in the Wastes.'

'Aye, he were for keepin the Devil from our shores, unlike ye, what hath calt filth and impurity upon us. Ye were tryin to prevent me from seein it, stopped me from venturin further along the shore for ye were hidin the Beastht from me!'

'Blather-spake, she werenoh yet upon the Quag. It were yer wee stone throwin and Grathican feet I were tryin to keep from these sands, yers and any other from the village.'

I begun movin twort the boy.

'Stay there from me!'

Steppin backwise he begun scowlin and snarlin like a deranged wee animal.

'Thou art the kin of the Beastht! Ye lie with Leviathan!'

Hurlin one last stone, the boy turnt and bolted down the sand.

I thought upon chasin after him but decided agin it, as it'd do me no good anywise. Instead I watched him disappearin in a distance, his wee scant legs pumpin the sand for all they was worth. When he were gone, I collected the sea in a bucket forta douse Levi. She had become silent and sombre and made no fuss as the water were throwt upon her.

'It will be knowt now,' sayt I, rubbin the brine into her flesh. 'All Grathico will soon know of yer arrival.'

I turnt from her, lookin down the shore at the mull over which the Stone Thrower had disappeared on his way back to the village.

It were nice while it lasted, sayt she with a wee mordant flip of the tail.

XI

It were his hand what come first, cane clasped within it, hoistin himsen upon the rocks – the gapin black sleeve of his cloak like a wee dark mouth. Next were the hat, wide-brimmed and made of leather, sittin firm upon his skull. A small figure scrambled up the mull and stood aside him, the Stone Thrower no doubt, him what'd run straight back to tell about the Leviathan. The Prelate turnt to look upon the boy who were leppin about and pointin at us like a mooncalf – it were then I saw the familiar jut of the long hooked beak of his mask, comin crooked and claw-like from aneath the hat.

It were sayt that since the Great Pestilence the beak bin filled with perfumes – rose petals and lavender and the like forta keep from inhalin the stench of death what bore the scourge from one soul to another. It were sayt the vestments worn by the Prelate bin passed down from his blood and kin from the time of the plague, when the Great Mortality reaped its harvest upon the dissolute souls of Ereb – that unholy mass of land what had broken away from the word of God and drifted twort Hell.

The Prelate's kin had tried to cure the sinful of their wickedness – some went with the Flagellants, crossin all Ereb repentin for the sins of man through the whippin and mortification of their own flesh. Some, such as the Prelate's father's father, had worn the vestments of the plague doctor. The cane they carried bin used to inspect the infected without havin to touch em and to keep souls at bay, for somespells the plague doctors were forced to beat their way out the houses and villages of the damned – clingin to their limbs or coat-tails the poorly and desperate pleaded for deliverance, for their own lives to be taken. It were to the Prelate – his blood and kin – that we owed the salvation of our souls, for when it were recognised there were no hope, that Ereb's drift twort Hell were irrevocable, they gathered the healthy and God-fearin and loaded em into boats. The Prelate were only a wee boy when his kin set their sails north, twort God, and away from the things of man.

Anywise, that boy had become a man and were now stood atop the mull starin upon me. The souls of the village swarmed around him, spreadin either side till they near covered its length. The Prelate were like a great black cormorant standin among em – a man-bird with his squawkin flock behind him, cep they was quiet enough truth be tolt, for the sight of the Leviathan had em mute and mumchanced. Raisin his cane skyward, he helt it there a spell afore whippin it down hard and fast so that it sat pointin square upon mysen and Levi. Same as the sea runnin her cold dark fingers through the rocks, the men what surrounded the Prelate poured down the cracks and clefts of the mull – comin upon the sand they begun their march twort us.

When they was about halfway they stopped, pullin up slow and nervous at the sight of her enormous sen stretched large and brazen upon the sand. *That's right*, thought I, *stop and take her in, be silent and humble afore her.* Restless and fidgety the men dithered some, unwantin to go fort, till the Prelate marched through em that is; with the boy and Closemen behind him he ploughed through the cluster of befuddled souls millin about aimless upon the shore. Hushed and sheepish, they followed his dark and silent sen with their eyes, till the Stone Thrower turnt upon em.

'Cowardth!' screeched the child, afore showin his back to em.

The Grathicans whispered among emsens a spell afore continuin on twort mysen and the whale. Withy's tall gangly sen moved out from the crowd – walkin to the side of the Prelate his stance were erect and ceremonious. Starin straight ahead he begun singin the 'Prelude', which were the song that announced the arrival of the Prelate into the church or whatsoever ceremony there may be. The men fell in line then, the song galvanisin and unifyin their spirits; every hand come to the face in the sign of the mask as they done at church when the Prelate entered.

His dark beaked sen wouldnoh look upon me, far as he were concerned I werenoh there, all his concentration were centred upon the Great Fish. His half dozen Closemen, the very same what I done the Thrum-Patter for, marched their hooded sens behind him, eyes turnt to the ground.

'How goes it?' whooped I, when they was in earshot.

Melas bit down hard and vicious upon the sand when I sayt that; I'd noticed her swellin and becomin more agitated the closer the men come, for she were none too pleased they was there neither. The Grathicans stopped to look upon the sea,

78

their pale faces wizened with fright. Ye'd have laughed some could ye seen em, shakin in their boots at the rancour of her dark and watery sen – mooncalves. Even the Stone Thrower were shaken, for I saw his wee ferocious frame blanch at the unexpected violence of the sea.

'That's right,' sayt I, 'ye have come upon hostile shores! Unbidden are ye and yers upon these sands!'

My hair bristled at the thrash and tumult of the sea – gooseflesh skittered up-a-down my spine as a deep well of violence settled snug-like in my belly.

'Melas has warned ye,' sayt I, pluckin a spear from the sand, 'now so have I!'

When they was close enough I hurled the spear into the air, aimin for the small cluster of men out in front – the Prelate and his Closemen – but it come up short and landed in the sand with a soft impotent thud. The men raised their weapons when I done that, ready forta riddle me with spears and fashion me in the likeness of old Saint Sebastian himsen, who were a favourite of the Prelate's, what with the arrows all through him and the great anguished expression upon his mug. Anywise, the Prelate gestured for the men to lower their spears – doin as they was tolt, the weapons come back to their sides and instead they tilted their bodies twort me. Pluckin another spear from the sand I moved out some and helt it across my chest, positionin mysen forta protect Levi. The Prelate stopped movin then and let his Closemen come fort; they was near enough so as to hear the sound of their boots slippin and squelchin in the sand. Aneath the shadows of their hoods I could see the stony faces, eyes unblinkin and fixed upon me. I thrust the spear at the first soul what come near and woulda caught him through his heart, cep for the fact he twisted himsen at the last moment. Grabbin hold of my spear, he broke it in two and struck me across the face. Three of em was atop me afore I even hit the sand, my hands were pulled tight agin my back as the weight of their bodies was throwt upon me. Strugglin, I spat and swore at em till a filthy paw were placed upon my skull and a sword agin my gullet. Approachin Levi, the Prelate begun movin round her, inspectin her so it seemed. Throstle were millin about sheepish-like in the crowd; orbs skittish, he peaked his skull out from inbetwix the limbs of the men, till he caught mine eye that is, whereupon he pulled his head in and disappeared back into the throng. Withy took up a place on his own, back some from the whale, ready to sing hymns of praise and supplication – for all his rigidness though, I could see he were desperate to glance upon me.

Somewise, I'd ended up twort the long block of Levi's skull what were at least five times the length of me. Her eye moved slowise and sluggish to look upon me – *We're done for now,* sayt she, *food for the fishes in the sea and the birds what circle above, I and ye. Mind, I'm none too nettled about it – I'm quite at peace with it mysen.* She sayt it all haughty-like, as though she were above feelin sorry for hersen, or mysen – like my qualmishness about mortality and impermanence were a great embarrassment to her. *Alright for thee,* sayt I, *naught to lose with thy great and colossal sen stranded upon this desolate shore, I on the other hand were yet to become a full growt wild thing, fierce and free.*

Whisht, sayt she, *stop yer whinin and bear it with grace for death is a lonesome dirge that a man must sing unto himsen.*

I thought upon what she sayt a spell. *That's noh bad Levi, wouldst thou mind if I used it in* The Philosophy of the Wastelands?

Thou shalt do as thou pleases, sayt she, *God knows.*

'Is it dead?' shouted one of the men. 'Is the Beast dead?'

The Prelate raised his cane forta silence him. Orderin the men to strip Levi of the blankets, he crouched down where her long tail begun, as though he were attemptin to look aneath her. Motionin for the Stone Thrower to join him, the two huddled in the sand – her large grey sen a wall of flesh behind em. The beaked mask covered the Prelate's whole face, there was two round glass panels for the eyes but when he spaked to the Stone Thrower there were no movement round the gob. The boy didnoh nod his skull or indicate anythin were bein sayt to him – it seemed as though they was doin naught cep crouchin afore the Leviathan, starin upon each other, silent-like.

After a spell they rose, the boy standin behind the Prelate so that he were covered by the long black cloak and couldnoh be seen by the men of the village. Still and all I, and the gowks what oppressed me, could see him standin there clear-as-ye-like. The boy, as First Stone Thrower, were chosen to be the Voice and would proclaim the words of the Prelate. The Voice allway had to be a Stone Thrower, on account of the fact they was pure enough to carry the Sacred Stones. None but the First Stone Thrower or the Closemen was allowed to hear the Prelate's true and proper voice, though I'd bin raised in his house a course and had heard him more-an I'd care to remember.

'No!' sayt the boy. 'It is noh dead! The Beastht doesnoh die – it is in a state of metamorphothith!'

Metamorphosis were what he meant when he sayt that. The Prelate kep still as his words were proclaimed while behind him the Stone Thrower's face become scrunched and venomous, spit flyin from his gob with the violence what coursed

81

through his tongue. Ye could see it near cost him his life to keep his hands by his side and noh move his body as he spaked the will of the Prelate.

'Hith unholy sen is among us! We must dethtroy the Leviathan afore it hath time to complete its tranthformation. The Beastht must be dethtroyed!'

The boy moved out from behind the Prelate and approached the Closemen what stood to the side of the crowd. He spaked in hushed tones among em afore they nodded their hooded skulls and moved off twort the others. I couldnoh hear what were bein sayt to the Grathicans, but soon as the Closemen finished they all turnt and walked back up the sand the way they come – a hundred and more souls movin down the shore, Withy's voice guidin and protectin em as they marched back twort the village.

'Where they off to then?!' enquizzened I of the Prelate.

I were answered none a course, cep by the boot of the Stone Thrower as he marched over and landed one in the gizzards – took mine air so it did.

'Brave thou art now, child, restrained as I am upon the sand by these gowks. Noh so brave this morrow though wert thee? All atremble with the fear thee wert then, ran thy feeble and delicate sen up the sand upon very quiversome pegs, if I mind well.'

He begun to march back twort me but the Prelate stopped him, placin his cane across the boy's very sensitive and prideful chest.

I were kep restrained upon the sand the whole longspell the men was gone. The Prelate hovered by the Leviathan, walkin round her but allway returnin to that same spot where her tail begun,

82

where her great body begun to narrow and taper some. All thoughtful and the like he rose from his haunches, turnt from the whale and stood contemplatin the sea. I watched his cloak billow in the breeze, the long crook of his beak appearin either side of his shoulders as he turnt this-way-a-that, lookin up-a-down the watery mass engirdlin the gullet of our barren ait.

The Prelate stepped back as the sea surged upon the sand, she'd bin nowhere near him, truth be tolt, still-yet he come back, makin as though it were sheer fortuity and chance that he'd retreated at the same spell as a fierce black wave come upon the shore.

'Thou hast made thysen a friend and cully there!' sayt I.

The beak come over the shoulder at the sound of my voice.

'Melas is awful fond of thee – sure and certain she is!'

I cackled some then, for I considered mysen amusin.

The Prelate turnt good and proper and, marchin his way over, crouched down so as he were near sat atop me – the brim of his hat blockin the sun, throwt the two of us into shade.

'Melas is comin for the Leviathian,' sayt I. 'She'll noh allow thy hands upon her.'

Aneath the mask, he took deep breaths through his neb. He were makin a point of it, so he were, raisin the long hook of his beak each spell he done it.

'The stench of the sea,' sayt he, 'the deaths of all those bodies still upon its breath.'

He come closer then, got nice and cosy agin me.

'The same smell is upon thy creature – it will soon be upon thee.'

Leanin in, the point of his beak almost touchin my skin, he sniffed some more.

'If it is not already.'

83

Noh even the men what had hold of me woulda heard him, noh in the whispers he were spakin, nor above the din Melas were makin. He were so close I could see the fine cross-stichin what ran down the centre of the mask and along the length of the hooked neb.

'It is true what thou says,' sayt I. 'The smell of death is upon me, for thou art close and I am wanin neath the foetor and tyranny of thy gull-breath.'

His eyes moved about behind the glass panels, blinkin the way they do when he were incandescent and seethin. It werenoh just the beak and the dark garms what made him resemble the cormorant but the iridescent watersome blue orbs – frozen and fathomless, a faint amber ring encirclin the pupil. The panels of the mask was larger-en his eyes and ye could see the dark and grey of his eyebrows and the deep lines etched upon his oldenin skin – he looked trapped in there, truth be tolt, as though he'd bin sown up inside the skin of another creature and couldnoh escape. Lowerin the point of his beak agin my face he ran it back-a-fort across the cheek – it were rough and sharp, and I felt it scratchin and cuttin into my skin.

'Ye have warned me?' sayt he, quiet-like, mockin me. '*Ye* have warned *me*?'

Diggin the hooked neb into my cheek he drew it hard across my face, slicin the skin as he rose and come upward upon the feet. The cane come down next, vicious-like into the sand, it caught the tip of my lug which I can tell ye is a fierce squishy and tendersome part of the skull. It pained me somethin awful and I couldnoh help but howl, for it felt as though it near bin tore clear off. I turnt back to curse upon him but saw only the swoosh of his cloak as he turnt and were gone.

84

'Here they come!' screeched the Stone Thrower, skull turnt down the sand. 'Come, the Grathicans!'

Grathicans sayt he, as though he werenoh one himsen, as though they was a different strain all agether. Withy's singin come trailin across the wind bringin the men upon it. Comin down the sand they carried somethin upon their shoulders, long poles so it seemed by the way they was marchin one behind the other in columns. Movin out to meet the men, the Closemen stood in a distance, a small truss of hooded souls gesticulatin with the arms and givin instructions.

There were heavy tackle swingin from the end of the poles like pendulums – pulley blocks they was, used for buildin and movin and the like. A soul at the front of the pole on the cliff side lost his footin and went down like a sack. The pulley block plummeted to the ground and brought the pole risin and liftin away from the shoulders of the men behind; slowise it pitched to the side and – near hittin the souls marchin alongside – it come down to the shore with a thud. There were hubbub and tumult then, much cursin and spittin as the men clustered at the front of the pole and lifted there, where the weight were. Pole upon shoulders they moved off again, sweatin and groanin and the like. Some souls had great lengths of rope wrapped round their bodies, others carried ladders of different shapes and kinds. Out in front the Stone Thrower had taken it upon himsen to direct the men – somespells walkin backwise, somespells frontwise, arms pointin this-way-a-that, he bawled orders like a wee tyrant conductin a burdened and beyoked crew of very sorry souls. As the Grathicans streamed past, mine orbs become fixed upon the smooth metal of sundry mean-lookin hooks, till I were yanked to the feet by the gowks above and dragged round the further side of the whale.

There were much activity happenin there already – Levi were bein measured from skull to tail in strides. The Prelate himsen were countin out paces then diggin the cane in and drawin a line away from her body, markin a spot whitherto the men scurried and begun shovellin into the shore. Six holes was dug, till the sand comin up were wet and sludgy and the men inside near vanished. Metal plates was lowered to the bottom and the long poles was brought over and fixed into brackets. Rocks, large and small, were packed round the base of the holes with wet and dry sand inbetwix, then more rocks and so fort, till they was smooth and level. The six long poles what come out the ground craned twort Levi, castin their slender shade across the shore like immense sundials.

Scaffoldin and ladders was brought in next, supports was mounted under the poles and the pulley blocks unfastened. Ropes was fed through the metal wheels from which men – two-a-time – swung back-a-fort, testin to see they helt good and proper. A ladder were laid agin Levi's flank, just behind her skull, and soon a Grathican were climbin the rungs with one of the cumbersome hooks clasped in his hand. Becomin level with her heighth he fastened the hook to the ladder and stared down at the dark and wet flesh aneath him.

'Walk upon the Beastht! Stand proud and firm upon the Devil!' bawled the Stone Thrower.

Dippin the beak, the Prelate gave a wee furtive nod and the man made to move out upon the whale, but it were as though his body forbade him and he slumped agin the ladder, embracin it like a child.

'Recreant! Coward!' screeched the boy afore the cane were brought down in front of him.

Leanin down, the Prelate whispered somethin to him, whereupon the boy jumped in behind the cloak.

'If thy feet donoh first tread upon the Beastht, they'll ner again walk upon the sand!'

The man's head sunk agin the ladder – considerin his fate, I expect. Climbin round to the innerside he come down a rung or two. Reachin out with one foot, he kep a tight hold upon the ladder – knuckles white and atremble. There werenoh a sound cep the sea lashin and bitin agin the shore as every soul upon the sand were still with what may happen next. As for mysen, I were burstin with glee, awaitin the wrath of the whale to waken and be brought upon their skulls. After a longspell, the foot come upon the wild and unmapped flesh of the Leviathan, whereupon it were retracted again quick-as-ye-like as though he thought his limb may burst into flame.

The man begun to say his prayers aloud and those aneath joined him;

'Though I walk through mist and shadow of death I fear noh evil, for thou art with me. Thy rod and thy cane comfort me. Father and Prelate, wash me with purest waters of repentance, prepare me to be allway a livin sacrifice unto Thee, who livest and reignest, upon world without end.'

The prayer were repeated till it become a chant what growt louder and louder, almost drowin out the sound of the sea. Behind the drone of the men, Withy's crystalline voice quavered in prayer, till the Stone Thrower come in with the old refrain;

'On earth ath it is in heaven!'

'As it is in heaven!' rejoined the men.

The child begun dancin round, singin and shoutin like a mooncalf.

'On earth ath it is in heaven!'

'As it is in heaven!'

The Prelate raised his cane into the air – the chant risin skyward with it.

Even the souls what had hold of me were shoutin their lungs out and near deafenin me. I felt my gizzards churnin and risin to my gullet, *Come on, Levi*, I were sayin to mysen, *bring Hell upon their skulls!*

'Fervour and Passion!' screeched the Stone Thrower, raisin his wee zealot's fist.

The cane come down then and the man, hallooin and bawlin, lep from the ladder onto the Leviathan thinkin he were throwin himsen into the great black jaws of Hell – a sacrificial lamb and all.

Naught, silence – chant dead, cane back in the sand and a man on his haunches atop a whale lookin about himsen as though unbelievin he werenoh burnin amid the eternal fires of damnation. It were as though every soul, mysen included, were surprised the heavens had noh descended, cep Melas a course, what kep hissin and laughin behind us – *What did ye expect? What did ye think may happen? Ha! Gowks and mooncalves the lot of ye!* The man lifted his hands from the Leviathan's flesh and stared upon em in wonderment. Turnin round he helt his palms out to the Prelate afore sweepin em slowise over the skulls gathered aneath – a great cry come from the men when he done that, and they raised their fists and spears and swords, shakin em twort the sky.

Risin to his feet, the man took the hook from the ladder and turnt to walk wee cautious steps across Levi's flesh. Movin as far across her as he could, he hoved it above his head and awaited the signal from the Prelate. *Wooooosh!* come the

88

sound of the cane as the man turnt from the Grathicans and swung with all he may into the body of the Leviathan.

I were concentratin upon her eye, upon that wee black stone to see somethin register, pain I spose – life. I'd bin expectin her mouth to open and pronounce a curse upon all the Quag. I were waitin to feel the thud of her tail through the sand, but there were naught cep the dull sound of the hook enterin her body and the tremor of her flesh as she absorbed the blow. Unfetterin a mallet from his belt the man crouched down and drove the hook deeper into her blubber – the hollow clinks of metal upon metal were swallowed by the mass and give of her flesh.

'Come on, Levi!' screeched I.

My pegs was swept from aneath me and afore I knowt it I were lyin upon the sand again.

'Make up yer minds,' sayt I to the gowks. 'I'm shoogly with the way ye have me up-a-down the wholespell.'

'Shut it!' I were tolt as they jostled me about, manhandlin me in such a way so as I were shakin in my boots at their very brave and fierce sens.

The rope from the pulley of the first pole were run up the ladder and attached to the hook with snug, tight knots – her flesh were tugged and pinched as the man pulled hard upon the rope till he were satisfied the hook were fixed proper. By the fourth hook he'd become brave and were walkin heavy upon the whale, jumpin up-a-down and kickin into her. He made a show of drivin the hooks in and enjoyed the clappin and shoutin from the cowards below. It were as though he were walkin upon me, I could feel the hooks bein driven into mine own flesh, twisted through mine own innards.

'Brave man thysen!' sayt I, my voice croakin and waverin like a child. 'I may walk upon thee a spell! I may take great pleasure in drivin hooks into thy flesh and stompin all over thee!'

I received a blow to the skull for my troubles; watchin my blood pool into a wee divot in the sand, I pondered the divergent and sundry cruelties what may be done unto a man.

Once the hooks was imbedded in her skin the cretin were bidden to come back down the shore and the ladder were removed. He took up position next to one of the poles while most the men divided into six clusters and stood aside the ropes. The pulleys was such that the best leverage were gained by drawin the rope inward, twort Levi. Standin with their backs to the beast the men took hold of the ropes – windin and meshin it round their arms, they turnt to look upon the Prelate.

'Pull!' screeched the Stone Thrower as the cane swung through the air.

A low groanin come from the men as they clamped down on the rope. The hooks bit into Levi, raisin her flesh into wee grey mounds, and slowise she begun to roll. Withy were stood on his own singin while Throstle were among those pullin at the ropes – his mug squishy and fretful at the great stress he were under while his short stubby pegs slipped and quivered in the sand.

'Pull!' bawled the Stone Thrower. Runnin and dartin betwix the ropes he barked at the men like a dog roundin sheep. 'Yaaah! – Hove up!– Pull!'

The wheels of the pulleys creaked as the rope inched through. Blood from Levi's wounds ran down her flank, snakin its way twort the sand. As she were rolled her flesh begun to give – the second hook down her body tore clear through her tough blubbersome skin and shot back twort the men. The rope spun and clattered through the pulley as those what helt it tumbled one atop the other into the sand. The hook shattered the supports of one of the poles and tore into the body of the man what stood aside it. I werenoh able to see the soul it struck but heard the shrill song of agony rattle through his lungs as he sunk into the sand.

'Pull!'

The remainin ropes come taut – the men leant back, muscles tremblin, foreheads scrunched and perspirin, till Levi come full on her side.

'Stop! Stop!' bawled the Stone Thrower, near leppin from his skin.

The Leviathan were on her flank and I could see the spout atop her skull what looked like an eye with the lid closed. Wooden stakes was driven into the sand and the ropes wound round forta keep her steady. Dragged to my feet I took no notice of the gasps and murmurs of the men as I were brought round to where they was all gathered, for I were too busy gawpin upon the pale expanse of Levi's vast belly and listenin to the holler and moans of the man what writhed in pain on the further side of the whale. *Aaaarrrrryyaaahhh! Mercy upon my soul!* screeched he and other such jarble and bother. Himsen, the beaked one, were back standin down the base of her tail, that part of her what so enthralled him.

The Prelate helt the cane across his body.

'Back!' shouted the boy. 'Back!'

Placin his wee Stone Throwin hands agin their stomachs the child drove the men back. It werenoh till they was dispersed that I understood – protrudin from the bottom of Levi's belly, near where her tail begun, somethin long and grey and flesh-coloured were swishin this-way-a-that.

Hersen, the Leviathan, were with child.

91

XII

'Preserve us!'
'Progeny of the Devil!'
'Brood of the Beast!'
'In His name!'
'His name!'
'His name!'
Such and other were the inanities and blather the Grathicans conjured in the great empty recesses of their skulls as they looked upon the half-born calf protrudin from the belly of its mother. The Prelate and Stone Thrower were huddled, conspirin afore the vast body of the whale.

'This is the metamorphothith upon which I warned ye!' sayt the boy, as he slipped behind the cloak. 'The Beastht is givin birth unto itsen, it shall multiply upon the sand afore movin over the Quag – gatherin the spirits of the Wastelands, it shall march upon the village and lay waste to Grathico. The spire of our church shall be in flames – its sacred walls shall become a kiln for the speckleth souls of our children.'

The Prelate pointed his cane twort me.

'This is the creature what has brought the Devil upon us! He hath invited the Beastht to our shores . . .'

I laughed some when he sayt that – like Levi were acceptin invitations and didnoh just go wheresoever she pleased. Thing were though, I'd bin musin upon this since Withy sayt it me atop the cliff and had begun to think they was half right. I'd bin doin more-an just sittin upon those rocks waitin for her. Standin there with the gowks hands upon me, squintin blood from the orbs and crunchin sand betwix the teeth, I realised I'd bin callin her a longspell – since I were a wean, like as noh. I'd bin callin that beast to me since the womb. In fact, it seemed my whole life bin that one word, that wee simple word – *come!* I'd sayt it over and over, I'd turnt it into song and cast it across the seas, across Melas' long dark spine. It were a provocation, more or less, a challenge to some distant thing – *come!*

I'd ner knowt what I bin callin to, I'd noh cared much, truth be tolt, it were more in the callin than anythin it may bring. I spose it were from a yennin that I'd sent my soul into the Wilds and calt upon distant creatures. The Prelate says yennin is the main ingredient of the Devil's tincture, if that be so then the Devil's tincture stirs deep inside my bones, it has become lodged there and turnt brittle and violent – it ails me some, makin me restless and bockety and the like. Yennin has allway played havoc upon my soul which only made me call harder. *Come!* I'd hissed from inside my mother's belly. *Come!* sayt I, with all the sorcery of my wee unborn soul – *and bring all Hell with ye!*

93

Thinkin upon it, it is a lonesome and somewise unrewardin way for a soul to spend his time, still-yet, I recommend it, in fact it come next in *The Philosophy of the Wastelands*; call blind-like unto the Wilds – from distant lonesome shores, cast yer spell upon the world. For those what have ears'll hear it, sure and certain – it is a song sung upon its own frequency, same as the Leviathan's, and those what donoh, well, that be their loss, for that be a fate lonesomer than the Wastes – that is an isolation my soul could ner know.

Course, it were possible I were wrong about the whys and wherefores of what brought Levi to our shores – praps she'd come cause I'd driven her pure demented with all my hissin and moanin and so fort. Like as noh I'd driven her clear out her senses with my very noiseful yennin and persistent spell-castin. Praps the Leviathan and her kind are fierce sensitive when it come to the sound of provocations issuin from distant shores. Praps it were like listenin to a whistle bein blown, high-pitched and squealy, straight into yer skull. Like as noh, it were a source of great distress to her. The Leviathan had come ashore out of pure desperation from listenin to the yelpin and moanin of my wee needy soul – *Shut it, O human child! Whisht there, O fierce wild beast-boy! Shut thy gob for yer moanin dost distress me.* Course, I can only surmise what were goin on inside her skull, that is only a proximation of the kind of thing the Leviathan may or may noh have bin thinkin as she come ashore to confront a beast-boy livin wild upon the Quag – that godforsaken island, somewhere north of Hell.

'He himthen is the progeny of the Devil ath is well knowt,' sayt the Voice. 'He were born backwise with the feet first like this creature is bein born – ath is the way of the Devil, whose blood he shares. The body of hith own mother couldnoh bare the evil inside it and she were torn apart by the corruption of his thrawn and forthcomin soul. He were seen this morrow lyin with the Beastht, stretched upon the ground like a dog at the feet of its master. He hath invited this thing upon us – he hath brought the Devil to our shores!'

It were true what the Stone Thrower sayt – I kilt mine own mother. I'd heard this story for as long as I could mind, himsen the Prelate had tolt it me as a boy – it were one of his favourite tales and he derived much pleasure in tellin it me over and over. He sayt I were born upsy-down with the feet first – inverted, so he calt it. When first I started comin into the world they thought my feet was the horns of the Devil, old Lucifer himsen comin straight out the womb of my mother – but it were just my feet and pegs is all, comin afore they spose to. It were a sign though he tolt me, a sign I were the kin of the Beast, that it werenoh only my body but my soul what were upsy-down. I cannoh disagree all agether about that, mostspells my soul feels like it's upsy-down, like it's dizzy some from standin on its head a longspell. Truth be, I'd allway bin in exile, even when I lived among em. On account of the fact I'd bin raised in the house of the Prelate and cause of all the stories surroundin my birth most Grathicans had kep their distance. I'd run with the weans as a whelp a course, led em, more or less, but as I growt older even they become remote. Anywise, for sundry and divergent reasons I'd bin considered a rare and prickly creature – noh that I'd ever done much to dispel the murmurs about me. A wee humble and misunderstood beast-boy was yers truly – poor thing.

'He were tryin to hide the Leviathan and allow it time to breed upon the Quag, to sow its wretchedneth into the soil.'

That were news to me.

'The Beastht and its bondsman shall lay waste to all we have built in Hith Holy name. We must dethtroy the malevolent creature afore it hath time to propagate.'

The Prelate raised his cane into the air.

'We must kill the Beastht what reside inside the Beastht!'

There were shouts of approval from the Grathicans.

'Kill the Beastht inside the Beastht!' bawled the child.

The roar of the men become louder and they begun to chant in unison.

'Kill the Beast inside the Beast!'

The boy sprung out from behind the Prelate – dancin and leppin about, whippin the men into frenzy.

'Kill the Beast inside the Beast!'

The Prelate motioned for em to be quiet, whereupon the Stone Thrower quit actin the mooncalf and slipped in behind the cloak.

'Who will claw the Beastht from itsen? Who will slay the child of the Devil?!'

A number of men stepped fort and the Prelate directed em to stand behind the calf. Its tail begun to wiggle and thrash and it were only after much effort that they was able to grab hold of it. The others stood at the ready, swords and axes raised above skulls. I begun threshin in the arms of the men what restrained me for the thought of em touchin Levi's calf near drove me wild.

'Take yer loathy, boggin hands from it!' bawled I.

The Prelate raised his arm.

'Kill the Beastht inside the Beastht!'

The cane were brought down and the men pulled back upon the tail – though, as soon as they begun hackin into the calf's unborn flesh, its mother's jaw fell open and there come from her an almighty and harrowin cry. Levi's yowl stunned the souls upon the sand who fell to their knees as though the sound had rendered em lame. The noise what come from her were ancient and stark, it were a squall of violent music what swept over the body and sent shards burrowin into the skin. A judgement had sounded from the belly of the whale, a howl had come from the cold black heart of the sea and it gave all the Quag cause to tremble.

Levi's great limb swung fort, ploughin through the men what were gathered there. The force of the blow sent em flyin like skittles and they was laid flat upon the sand. Another hook down the end of her body come free – tearin through her flesh it sprung back and disappeared behind her. I were mumchanced, truth be tolt, for I thought she were gone, I'd dared noh say it to mysen but I thought Levi were gone from us. Some of the men upon the sand were attemptin to crawl away on hands and knees, others whimpered and whined as they clutched different parts of emsens – a number lay still and didnoh move at all. I cheered then, a cry of pure joy lep from me as I watched the men slitherin like worms.

'That's it, Levi!' bawled I. 'That's it!'

As though she were answerin me, there come a great blow of air soundin from atop her skull.

'Blood!' screeched a voice. 'Blood!'

Some of the men had sneaked to the further side of the whale forta avoid the wrath of mother and child.

'The Beast breathes blood!'

Lookin up I saw a faint red cloud waftin twort us, the feathersome whits and jots lifted by the wind and blown across her body – some of the wee pink beads settled upon her, glistenin in the sun like a lather of sweat upon her skin. The men what

97

come round from the further side were slabbered with gore, one were head-a-toe and drippin with it – holdin his arms wide, the whites of his orbs gleamed with terror as he looked down upon himsen, horror-stricken and mute.

In a panic, the men backed away; shoutin and yellin they throwt their weapons at Levi and turnt to run back up the sand. The Prelate stood firm and swung his cane at the first man what come past him – turnin to his side he filched a sword from one of the Closemen and drove it into the stomach of the soul he'd laid upon the shore. The men what saw stopped in their tracks and ran no more, those what had gone further soon realised none were followin and turnt to find the Prelate and the others starin after em – meek and slow, they begun to return. Leanin in, his dark sen whispered into the lug of the Stone Thrower and, quick as-ye-like, the boy were behind the cloak.

'Any man what flees shall be executed upon his return to Grathico!'

The Prelate turnt and headed back to Levi. Replacin the bloody and injured, he chose from among the cowards that had fleed to resume butcherin the calf. They was reluctant to approach a course, but it were that or meet the sword. Gettin hold of the calf were near impossible on account of the blood and the squirmin of the creature what had become half insane with fear.

'Kill the Beastht inside the Beastht!'

The boy's voice rang out round the cliff then sank into silence for the men kep quiet this spell, shoutin and jeerin none as the gowks begun pullin and hackin into the calf. It were maddenin to watch the creature bein slaughtered without the sound of struggle comin from its gob. I imagined I could hear it screamin and wailin inside its mother, mouth open, cryin bloody murder into the darkness of the womb. How could such a creature understand what were happenin upon it while its head were still encased in the shadowsome, dwam-makin darkness of its mother's belly? In another world, aneath the surface of the sea, that calf would've bin born a king, instead its mother bin washed upon the shores of the Quag and it were bein butchered by dim mooncalves what werenoh worth its spit.

'Come on, Levi!' bawled I. 'Kill the beasts what harm thy child!'

My voice sounded strange, as though I were a fierce upset wee child mysen. It were the slaughter without sound what got me. I promised mysen one thing, sure and certain – when my time come I'd noh go easy or quiet-like, when my time come I'd bring the skies with me.

'Come on, Levi!'

The flat of the blade were brought agin my skull but that stopped me none and I kep bawlin and hallooin. Keepin the orbs upon Levi I looked for a sign that she were still among us, but she'd become eerie still and quiet and, truth be tolt, I knowt she were gone.

Slippin out in a sudden, the calf come free of its mother – one of the men were unable to move from under it and the two fell slithery and viscous upon the sand. Fluids come after it, the dark tissue what had nourished it in the womb. The man begun squealin and wrigglin like a deranged thing – in shock he were, unable ado aught cep hold his skull and shriek as though his life were come to an end. I were surprised to see the calf still movin; thrashin its tail about it managed to wallop the man in the face a few spells afore slidin off to flip and flail its body some more. It were a strange sight, watchin the man and the creature writhin and cryin agether upon the sand, for it were then I first heard its voice – soft, feeble bleat-ins comin from its wee scared gob. Contortin and twistin its lacerated body, the calf drummed its blood into our shores.

The Prelate marched twort em, bringin a flurry of blows upon the man for makin a show and noh takin control of himsen. With tears streamin from his orbs the hysterical soul turnt onto his stomach – blatherin muzzy jarble he tried to crawl away from Levi and her calf. Followin him, the Prelate lashed the cane upon all parts – across his legs and shoulders afore landin a couple of fierce blows to the back of his skull, whereupon the man slumped into the sand and were uncon-scious. The Prelate took to the calf then, poundin its skull with his cane till the black wood become red.

'Coward!' I yelled him. 'Rakehell and coward!'

He stopped what he were doin and turnt to me; motionin for the men to bring me close he plunged the cane into the sand near the neb of the calf. I were dragged over and laid aside it, a boot placed upon my cheek so as I couldnoh look away. I stared upon the creature's large pink tongue as it opened and closed its gob, tryin to catch its breath. Eyes wild and dark, it looked about itsen in pure terror – *What Hell be this? What bleak, pitiless Hell be this?*

The Prelate stopped and looked around at the men what had become taciturn and inward. Raisin his arm he pointed the tip of his bloody cane at Withy, directin him forta sing. To the sound of the calf thrashin its flesh agin the shore, Withy opened his gob – frangible and resonant, his voice wove round the bowed skulls of the Grathicans as the Prelate turnt back to his base and bloody task.

His merciless sen continued to thrash the creature long after it stopped movin, long after it stopped cryin. The cane were still bein brought upon it even though its eye had burst and its wee soft mind were spilt upon the sand. He started with the boot then, bringin it down upon a skull what were already shattered and broken. Draggin the sword from the belly of the soul he'd slain, the Prelate begun sawin the calf's head free of its body. Bespattered with blood, he beckoned men to his side and had em thread spears through its jaw. With souls either end, the skull of the desecrated creature was raised upon their shoulders and marched back into the crowd.

After conferrin with the Prelate, the boy jumped behind the cloak.

'The body shall be throwt back to the sea, Melas shall know what happensth to those what attempt to harm the God-fearin souls of Grathico!'

Men from the crowd were mustered to lift the calf's body; slippin ropes underside its belly it were raised and cast into the sea. Upon their return the Prelate come over to me – a spider web of blood gathered at the tip of his beak, ripenin into a droplet it fell and spattered upon my cheek. Placin his cane aside my face he made a show of the blood what soaked it. I turnt my skull away but he brought it that side as well, I turnt again and he done the same. Motionin for the men to drag me in front of Levi he used the bloody end of his cane to draw a crude line of red streaks and smudges down the long white belly of the whale afore callin upon a soul from the crowd. The blacksmith were a large thewy man what had made himsen a fine and ornate sword, and it were for these reasons he'd bin calt upon. Sensin what were comin, I begun wrigglin like the devil aneath the Prelate's boot. My distress pleased him no end but he kep silent, starin down upon me with the feminine orbs what peeped out from behind the glass.

'Thou art the Devil!' I tolt him. 'It is ye who is the Beast, and I allway knowt it!'

The blacksmith were directed to stand afore Levi – placin the point of his blade agin her flesh he drove the sword deep into her belly. When the blade were sunk to the hilt he turnt and – placin both hands on one side of the helve – he dug his boots into the sand and drove the sword down the length of her gut.

The blade come through her chest, through her belly, down near where she'd birthed – rare thing were though, as the sword tore through her flesh naught come from her insides. Withy stopped singin, murmurin and unrest rose among the men but the Prelate were quick to hush em. Hand upon sword, the blacksmith turnt to see what his work had drawn fort but saw only the crooked wound where the sword had come through her. Slowise, the Prelate begun to approach the slain beast for a hummin were soundin from within her, a whirrin had begun inside her belly. Wide-eyed, the Grathicans looked upon one another with dread and disquiet.

The low rumblin inside her were risin and buildin to a pitch; coverin their ears the men begun backin away. The noise become unbearable even to mysen but I werenoh able to cover the lugs on account of the fact the gowks still had mine arms pinned behind my back. Just when I thought mine eardrums may burst, things become silent. There were gaspin then, *ooohhhs* and *aahhhs* comin from the men, and I turnt to see their outstretched arms pointin to Levi's chest where the blacksmith first drove his sword. Restin there, a large lone butterfly, the size of a man's hand, were sittin calm-as-ye-like upon the fleshy lips of the Leviathan's wound. Silent-like, it opened and closed its large luminous wings – *Howbe, lads?* it were sayin, cheeky some and brazen. Afore any soul had time to say aught, the sound inside Levi started up again and the men begun backin away. It were then, as they were retreatin with the wee backwise steps, that her stomach come open – still-yet, it werenoh her gizzards what spilt into the sand, it werenoh the Leviathan's slithery entrails what come from inside her, but a great flutterin of wings. A horde and plague of insects were streamin from the belly of the beast and had souls goggle-eyed and mute. The men froze and – gobs open like mooncalves – a hundred and more skulls tilted twort the heavens. The hooked white neb of the Prelate come skyward too, watchin as a deluge of butterflies poured from the Leviathan's belly and formed a darkenin cloud what gathered over the Quag.

A smile spread across my face at the sight, a warmth and joy whirred and hummed in mine own belly. The sound of em were bewutherin, like a great gush of water comin from inside her – *Shshshshshshshsh!* They looked like that and all, an upsy-down flutterin torrent of water flowin backwise into the sky – *Shshshshshshshshshsh!* Head buried in his hands, the blacksmith curled himsen round the helve of his sword what were still lodged in Levi's flesh. Peepin out at the men, he followed their stares skyward and spied the butterflies mushroomin into the heavens – fallin agin the whale, he slid down her belly afore crawlin away from her and disappearin into the crowd.

'The souls of the dead!' come a voice among the men. 'The Beast has dredged the souls of Ereb from the darkness of the sea!'

Forgettin emsens the men what had hold of me loosened their grip and, needin no invitation, I lep to the feet and hoofed it twort Levi. Standin in front of her, my lugs become filled with the sound of the frantic quiverin life what poured over me – *Shshshshshshshshsh!* Turnin round to face the men, I saw em lookin at me with jaws open and orbs half out their skulls. I watched their mugs blacken as the cloud of butterflies bloomed in the sky and growt across the sun, throwin the Quag into shade.

'The Darkenin!' come a voice. 'Eclipse and Darkenin!'

Neither the Prelate nor the boy sayt aught, but stared upon the sky.

In the crowd I spied Withy who were full of fear and tremblin – *What hast thou done?* he were sayin with the orbs. Keepin the skull skyward, Throstle wove through the bodies to snuggle and shiver agin his tall and gangly cully. I lifted mine arms what were laden with wings, for some of the butterflies saw fit to stop there and go no further. I were near covered with em truth be tolt; standin there with the arms and legs splayed, I looked like a garish quiverin star in front of a giant fish – a sight I were, sure and certain. The Prelate were stood right in front of me and so I raised mine arms higher and smiled upon him. The sight of my lips curlin near drove him wild and he charged fort and struck me across the cheek with his cane. The butterflies come away from me then, shatterin into a thousand wee and vibrant pieces.

Lyin across the sand I stared up at the sky and watched the flutterin cloud above movin as though it were one creature. It were like the butterflies was colludin with somethin on the ground or in the heavens for, in a sudden, they swooped down upon the Quag, descendin upon the Prelate and his men.

I couldnoh stop smilin truth be tolt, I were become a dozy mooncalf what couldnoh stop smilin as I watched em comin for me – *Come!*

The men begun shoutin and scatterin down the sand.

'Stand yer ground!' sayt the Stone Thrower. 'Stand agin the Beastht, cowardth!'

The hooked snout of the mask were skyward, watchin the creatures comin down upon him.

'A curse is upon ye!' bawled I, just afore they swarmed him, afore the Stone Thrower and all the men of the village were smothered by a plague of butterflies and forced to retreat. 'A curse is upon ye!'

Aneath the crush of colour, betwix the tumult of butter-fly wings, the white mask moved through the melee, blood streaked across its beak. Crawlin twort me, the Prelate's gloved fingers moved clumsy-like over my mug. Turnin my skull, I manoeuvred his fingers into my mouth and bit down hard as I could upon em. A muffled cry come from behind his mask then, and he brought his cane through the butterflies, vicious-like, forta batter my skull.

XIII

Wakey wakey there, beast-boy, time to gather those young and very troubled bones of yers.

That were Melas callin me back from the blackness, draggin me from the dark and voluptuous world into which I'd sunk after the Prelate clobbered me senseless. All kinds of delirium had bin swirlin about the brain in my torpor, butterflies mainly, swishin round the skull. The Prelate were there too, standin tall and thin with the mask and hat, the end of his cane buried in the sand, butterflies swarmin about him. I could feel his eyes burrowin into me, burnin in the pit of my belly. I thought he were death itsen come forta visit me, till I heard Melas callin that is, till her potent salty breath brought me to, lettin me know the Prelate and all Grathicans were well gone and it were just she and me, the butterflies and Levi stretched upon the shores of the Quag.

Rise and shine, beast-boy, the world is noh yet tired of yer wild and ferine ways. There are savage great accomplishments what lie dormant within ye. Melas knows, sweetin-child, she sees potential within ye – there is much potential what residith in yer bones, O fierce beast-child of the Wastelands.

I ignored her watery sen's mordant comments upon my person, instead I listened to her waves lappin in the neaptide, noh far from my feet. Melas were movin upon us, in sympathy praps, reachin out to mysen and the Leviathan in our spell of misfortune. I kep the orbs closed, for I werenoh as yet prepared to open em – somespells it is best to keep the eyes shut till the last possible moment, somespells wakin and seein is an inadvisable and unprofitable thing – so sayeth *The Philosophy of the Wastelands*.

The sun flittered through the lids – bright then dark, bright then dark, rhythmic-like and constant – it were the wings of a butterfly a course, openin and closin atop the skull, on the front there, the forehead and bridge of the neb. Listenin to the faint dronin of their flutter and carry-on, I could feel the creatures all over me, repositionin emsens as they battled with each other for the very sacred ground upon my gullet or forearm or whathaveye.

Chary-like, I opened an eye to the intricate patterns of a veiny translucent wing what were like a second eyelid, an extra layer protectin my very sensitive sight from the ungodly and distressin world beyond. Peelin back some, it allowed wee vicious fingers of sunlight to pour through and claw at the corners of mine orbs. Sittin bolt upright, the butterflies scattered as I rubbed the eyes good and proper, squintin and groanin and the like. I were fierce shoogly and had to put the hands down forta steady mysen. Melas were in front of me

107

a course, all bockety and askew, her smooth black tongue rollin twort me at queer, slopin angles. I sat there a spell – unmovin – waitin for the world to become moored and true.

Turnin to Levi, I saw she'd become a great mass of flutterin wings – covered from head to tail she were, with butterflies spreadin out along the ground betwix and beyond us. It were sayt that the unresolved souls of the dead, those spurned by God and the Devil alike, inhabited the form of a butterfly. Unable to ascend to the kingdom of heaven, nor be cast into the pits of Hell, they was sentenced to flutter about in purgatory for all eternity. There was no butterflies on the Quag and most souls had ner seen one, cep those what bin alife durin the time of upheaval and migration. All Grathicans knowt what they looked like though, on account of the fact his dark and holy sen kep a specimen trapped in a jar and locked away in the sacristy.

The Prelate sayt that as he and his kin sailed from Ereb they'd watched a horde of butterflies plumin into the sky, the souls of the damned fleein the flames of God's holy wrath. He sayt that one of the creatures become caught in the fire – wings singed, it fell from the sky and settled upon the deck of the ship where it were gathered into glass by his kin to remind souls what happens to those what stray from the Word. The butterfly were only brought out for rare and special ceremonies as it were considered one of the sacred chattels. A butterfly, sayt the Prelate, were a symbol of the end of days, a harbinger of iniquity and darkness.

I'd allway bin fascinated by the creature in the jar, unbeknowt to his holy sen I would sneak the key from his hangin garms and slip into the sacristy to gawp upon it. Spinnin the glass in my hands, I studied the frayed and blackened edges of its wings and the delicate antennae what sprouted from its skull. I were possessed by it, truth be tolt, for what reason I couldnoh say, but it were for allway on my mind. It were on account of the butterfly that I'd ended up in the Wastes – I woulda ended up here one way another, but it were my fascination with the trapped and colourful creature what at last drove me out the village. For one day – without my plannin it so – studyin the butterfly werenoh enough. I'd wanted to feel the weight of its feathery body in my palm and trace the jagged edges of its wings with my fingers – so I'd smashed the glass and taken it in my hands. All Hell broke loose when I were discovered a course, himsen becomin unhinged with rage and sickin his gowks upon me.

Scramblin out the church, Grathican skulls had swung thisway-a-that as I scurried through the streets – the Prelate and his men close behind. Comin to the limits of the village the they begun slowin up, thinkin I were trapped and wouldnoh go further, but I lep straight into the Fens and didnoh stop till I were in the Wastes proper, from where I saw the Prelate performin the rites over the men so as they could come after me. Stoppin mid-sacrament he swung the beak to look upon me and we each become still – the gowks, the Prelate and I – oglin each other till I turnt my back to em and ran deep into the Wastes. They ner did come after me, the Prelate musta decided agin it. A test I spose it were; he'd wanted to see how I'd fair on mine ownsome with naught but spirits for company.

Inland I'd come across the bothy, lonesome and rickety in the Wilds – its creaky door swingin back-a-fort, usherin me inside its damp and eerie numbles. I spent that first night shivery and afeared, spirits of the Wastes rattlin the bothy as I

109

huddled in the corner, holdin the butterfly in my hands like a hesitant and half-formed prayer.

Anywise, sittin upon the shore, starin at the butterflies what covered the sand betwix mysen and the whale, I considered what the Grathican had sayt about Levi dredgin the souls of Ereb from the bottom of the sea. I conjured images of her prowlin the ocean floor with her great gob open, gatherin the unresolved souls what had throwt emsens into the water, desperate forta climb aboard the ships of the Prelate and his kin. I were fond of the idea of Levi gluttin hersen on lost souls languishin in the silent blackness of the sea. I imagined her roamin the depths, belly hummin and whirrin with great satisfaction as they changed and fluttered about inside her. To be honest though, I cared naught from where and how the creatures had come – that they had come were what mattered to me.

I got on all fours and crawled twort the sea; cuppin Melas' cool and salty sen betwix the fingers, I splashed her upon the face, revivin mysen a tittle. Slowise I rose to the feet, butterflies partin afore me as though I were Moses himsen – twirlin up and around in funnels either side, like dust devils cep made out of wings. When I come to Levi, the butterflies settled some and I looked down the length of her very changed sen. Wings of different shapes and sizes opened and closed upon her, the blacksmith's sword, now covered with the creatures, still jutted out from the bottom of her belly. Other oddments come from her as well, the spears and axes what the men had throwt at her in their retreat. Butterflies sat upon her open gob and quivered all up-a-down her flank, they clung to the gapin wound of her belly and passed blithesome-like betwix her insides and outsides as though she were a great and fleshy cave. I moved round her tail to where the poles were – some toppled, some standin. The ropes what remained taut from the hooks in her blubber were covered in wings as well, strings of butterflies comin away from her, swingin some in the breeze.

I near tripped over the ladder what bin used to put the hooks in her flesh; draggin it from aneath the wings I rested it agin her back and climbed atop her. It were queer bein up there, things looked different, sure and certain, I could see down the sand to the mulls what enclosed us and felt the still-ness of her flesh aneath me. I spied the blood what had come from the spout atop her skull – the flecks and spatterins of red purged from her body as her lungs collapsed. I become still and starin upon that great V of blood, the shape of her vitality and mortality stretched upon the sand; it were the imprint of her last anguished breath, the stain of her contempt blown violent-like across the shore. On the further side were the men what bin kilt by the batterin of her powerful limb; one, what seemed to have no injuries, were curled into him-sen like a bairn wrapped snug in a womb of wings. The others lay bloody and broken – their bodies, and a wee slip of sand around em, were clear of the butterflies what wouldnoh go near em. From atop Levi, I looked down upon the men lyin still and frozen – slumberin constellations in a dappled sky of shudderin wings.

One of the butterflies plopped itsen square upon mine arm – facin me it twitched its antennae some.

'Thou hast bin inside the belly of the beast,' sayt I. 'What's that like then?'

Movin cautious across Levi's flesh, I minded to step over the ropes what come away from the hooks. Shufflin twort her neb, I noticed the only part of her that werenoh covered with wings were the dull black stone of her eye. I'd to get down on the hands and knees as I moved out upon her, for her skull were at a slopin angle. With the legs straddled either side, I placed the hands out in front and pulled mysen along thatwise. Her orb were much bigger-an I thought once I were close; placin the palms flat agin her, I begun strokin the tough wrinkled skin what surrounded it.

'I'm gonna take the hooks from thy flesh, if thou doesnoh mind?' sayt I.

Though, truth be tolt, I didnoh move for a longspell, but stayed there with my hands upon her, lookin at mine own very sorry skull what stared back at me from the darkness of her eye. In the end though, I did rise forta do as I sayt, slidin the rump backwise and gettin to the feet. Thing were though, when I got down on the haunches to pull the hooks out I found they was impossible to wrest from her skin. One after the other I tried but they wouldnoh budge. After near breakin the back with the effort I gave up, furious I were and woulda kicked em if it werenoh for the fact they was lodged in her flesh. Turnin away in a huff, I again spied the bodies of the men surroundin her what made me angry-some, sure and certain, for I didnoh like to look upon em and thought em somewise pollutin. Comin back down the sand, I took a shovel from aside one of the poles and dug a grave near the cliff away from Levi – one by one, the men was dragged by the ankles and rolled into the pit.

I were exhausted when I were done and fell to the knees all shivery and feversome. With the cold sweat runnin down my back I crawled twort Levi, twort her belly near where her calf bin torn from her. Clamberin inside her still warm sen, I wrapped my young and weary bones in her flesh and made like I were her calf. Inside her, I squealed and bleated the way the calf done as it were bein slaughtered, the same sounds I imagined it'd made inside the womb as the men hacked into its tail. I thought hard upon the calf as I bleated and bawled – squeezin the eyes shut I could still see the axe hewin into its unborn flesh.

I felt safe and warm in there, imaginin I were the child of that great and slaughtered beast. That is noh somethin I expect ye to understand – how could ye? Somewise, it is cause ye donoh understand that I'm here in the first place, laid up inside the Leviathan, pretendin to be her calf. I'm none too sure how that works, it is a suspicion let's say, but sure enough there is a connection. That's no souls fault a course and, truth be tolt, I wouldnoh be anywhere else. This is my rightful place, it is my home here, inside the belly of the beast with the butterflies roamin about her innards and flutterin all playful and skittery about my skull. Truth be tolt, one way another, this is where I allway bin, curled up inside the fleshy cave of the Leviathan – bleatin into darkness.

XIV

I'd taken the sword into the whale and were snuggled up agin it – flat of the blade pressed to the face so as to feel the smooth metal, cool and soothin upon the skin. In a distance, betwix the flesh and bone of the Leviathan, I spied a figure approachin. Wigglin fort, I saw a sable black dress trawlin itsen through the sand twort me. It were an oldenin Grathica, for she wore the white blouse of those beyond childbearin. I were surprised some, sure and certain, for woman and her kind werenoh bidden to wander about the Wastes as their spirits were deemed so feeble that noh even blessins could protect em. *What now?* thought I. Wearisome and grumblin, I slithered my heavy and reluctant bones from Levi's squelchy numbles. The woman swithered some when she saw me descendin the gut of the whale – *Donoh be alarmed*, sayt I, quiet-like inside the skull, *tis only my wee fearsome and beast-like sen slippin from out the belly of the Leviathan.*

114

Squintin some, I saw it were the old crone hersen come forta visit me, she of the baskets of slops and the day what clings to her and so fort. Praps she'd come forta lay stale bread and rotted fruit afore the Leviathan – *Hail, O Great and Mighty Fish, please accept my humble offerins of muck and rot.* She unnerved me some this woman, I'd allway bin suspicious upon her, even afore I come to the Wastes. She'd bin my shadow for allway, followin me round the village, leerin and gawpin at me from across the pews at church or in the streets and markets – allway with the beady old orbs upon me. As a whelp, I'd once chased her through the streets, for I didnoh like the way she looked upon me. Gatherin the other weans about me I'd hurled whatsoever were at hand, stones and bird skulls and such. Then, when I were older and lullin bout with Withy, I'd stopped her in the market.

'Upon what dost thou gawp, mother? Tis unpolite to stare upon a soul – hast thou noh bin taught?' But she'd become all shamefaced and ablushed and scuttered away from me.

'Who is this woman?' sayt I to Withy.

'Thou knows who she is, the midwife, a witch of sorts, doused in feminine sorcery.'

'She is allway leerin upon me.'

'Perhaps she means to lay a curse on ye with her old and evil orbs.'

'She is late for that, Withy, for thou art my curse. Thy long and gangly sen is my cross to bear in this world.'

Withy humphed when I'd sayt that, he were none too impressed, truth be tolt.

'She birthed me then?' enquizzened I, watchin as her bow-legged and irregular gait disappeared into the village.

'Ye and half of Grathico. Sure, ye knowt as much.'

'I'd ner thought upon it afore.'

'What's to think?'

'Naught, I spose.'

'Forget the old woman, she's no concern of yers.'

But I didnoh forget and took to spyin on her mysen. I followed her home once, peerin into her bothy as she were stooped over, stirrin her potions. She caught me lookin in at her and I were forced to retreat, scurryin back to the village all mortified and ashamed. I stayed clear of her after that. From then on we regarded each other with much caution, very intentional we were noh to look upon each other when our paths crossed in the village.

Anywise, here she were again, the old rickle of bones what had brought me into the world, watchin me be born again from the bowels of the beast. I were all goopy and slathered with Levi's innards – sword in hand and glistenin with viscera, I come upon the shore like a creature born to war, steppin fort from some innominate hell. The old one's fingers were fidgety and entwined and ye could see it took near everythin she had noh to turn and run back up the sand, or whatsoever it is these old ones do when they try to run – lollop I spose, flounder some and lurch.

The butterflies rose behind me as I moved across the shore. The pain in my bones were soothed by the hum and flutter of wings sweepin into the air – *kitter-katter-kitter-katter-kitter-katter*. The sound werenoh as furious as when they come from Levi's belly but still they loomed agether in great droves. The crone raised her skull, watchin the sallow sky blush with the mote shades of countless butterflies.

'What rare and perplexin treat be this?' enquizzened I.

She crinkled her forehead – more-an usual that is – lookin upon me as though I were spakin another tongue all agether.

116

'What brings thy hunched and wizened sen to the wilderness and the Wastes?'

She made to come closer.

'Thou needs come no further!' Grathicans arenoh welcome here! Ye can state thine ancient purpose, thine oldenin and feminine intentions, from afar.'

My voice were haughty, it were deep and boomin and were intended to instil fear in whomsoever heard it – *Butterflies and beasts rule here!* I were as much sayin.

'Thou canst pass on his message from there,' I tolt her.

'I've come with no message from the Prelate.'

'He knows thou art here?'

'No soul knows I'm here.'

'Thou hast bin blessed?'

'No.'

'No?'

'Blessins are no currency for woman and her kind, well thou knows.'

'Thou wilt noh survive without the blessin.'

'I will noh survive with the blessin.'

'Truth itsen.'

The old mother eyeballed the blade in my hand.

'Donoh let the sword nettle ye – tis only for show.'

She looked at me slantwise and unbelievin.

'I'm qualmish more for thy creatures than thy sword – I'm noh afeared of thee.'

'That so?'

'So it is,' sayt she, all steadfast and resolute.

Holdin her head erect she swept the grey hairs from her face so as to fix me good and proper with her fearsome, spirit-shakin old orbs.

117

'What brings thee here?'

The crone jutted her chin at Levi.

'It will do thee no harm, Prelate has seen to that.'

'He's comin for ye,' sayt she. 'I'm come to tell ye so. I heard it mysen, they are comin forta do ye harm.'

'To kill me, is what thou means.'

Turnin to the sea she nodded her skull.

'I knowt that already. They would have kilt me afore if it werenoh for the butterflies. Thou needst noh have sullied thy dress traipsin through the Wastes to tell me that.'

Her oldenin frame flinched some.

'Thou hast noh marched thine ancient bones through the Wilds to tell me that, hast thou mother?' sayt I, cockin the skull and lookin at her like I were a right clever beast-child what werenoh born yestermorn.

'Among others, I come to tell ye that. I come to tell ye the men of the village donoh want to return, they say the Leviathan and the butterflies are signs ye are protected by the Devil himsen.'

'Praps they're right. What dost thou think?'

She turnt her face skyward, lookin at the butterflies what hovered above.

'Is it true they come from inside the Leviathan?'

'Aye.'

'Then I donoh know what to think. Ye have some days, there is resistance but it willnoh last, he will persuade em the manner he allway do. The First Stone Thrower demands blood and retribution – he says heaven should be brought upon yer head.'

'He were unknowt to me till recent, who is the boy?'

'Devil-wean, thing possessed, conjured from the womb of some unfortunate forta enact the will of the Prelate.'

118

'His gob?'

'Poured boilin water down his own throat,' sayt she. 'Disfigured his face forta humble himsen afore God. It is sayt he blasphemed and for penance scolded his own tongue, purged it free of sin. His words were affected, it were sayt his tongue become burnt and melted to the side of his mouth and had to be cut away by the Prelate himsen.'

'Many things are sayt.'

'The boy himsen sayt it were the merciful hand of God and noh his own what poured the water upon him, what bathed his lips in repentance and scorched his tongue with compassion. He sayt it were the hand of God Himsen what learnt his soul the sting and rapture of His almighty grace. He sayt the thirst it quenched werenoh of the body but of the soul.'

'A vessel, sure and certain.'

She become quiet then, lookin past me.

'Can I see?' sayt she, noddin at Levi.

Afore I could say aught she were past me and next the whale. Keepin the eye upon her I stayed close as she walked around the Great Fish. The crone were very curious and studied every mark and scratch like she were some kind of sage on beasts what come from the sea. She stopped circlin and made to put her hand upon Levi's flank but, quick-as-ye-like, I lowered the sword and startled the old woman who almost become unwrinkled, such were the fright she took. The butterflies had growt wild, swarmin and flutterin round her, batterin her face and skull.

'Thou hast forgotted thysen, mother! Thy fingers shall noh know the flesh of the beast.'

The crone dared noh raise a hand agin the butterflies even though they kep rammin her skull. She were tryin to keep

119

calm but they unnerved her some and she become shivery and afeared.

'Remain still,' I tolt her.

She did as I bade and after a spell the butterflies settled.

'Thou shouldst noh be here. Unwanted are ye with yer mischief and devilry.'

She become silent and sulky as a child – shrinkin into hersen, she slunk off, shufflin round the Great Fish.

'Thou wert inside it,' sayt she, all hushpery with the eyes lowered – humility itsen, so she were.

'Aye,' sayt I, bit cold-like.

She kep circlin the Leviathan, that great cathedral of flesh and bone illuminated in part by the sun like candelabra bin hung in the nooks and crevices of its innards. Stoppin at Levi's open maw the crone stuck her head inside, evictin the butterflies what bin perched there. Takin deep breaths through her neb, she begun educatin me on the plight of the whale.

'It has started to perish,' sayt she, her voice deadened by the hollow of its flesh.

I kep quiet, for I were watchin the butterflies creep inside the long wound of Levi's belly. When the crone turnt her skull to look upon me, a glut of wings poured from the Leviathan's mouth causin her to squawk and fall back upon her oldenin rump. I couldnoh help but titter as I watched the butterflies rise into the air, the boldest few hangin about to harass the old woman as she rose to her knees. Dustin her hands she made a face as though she'd bin chewin on somethin very sour and unpleasant.

'Thou dostnoh learn, dost thou, mother?'

'I seen this creature afore.'

'Hast thou?' sayt I, very haughty and unbelievin.

'Aye.'

'It bin circlin the Quag.'

'No,' sayt she, 'afore, long afore.'

'Praps ye swum upon the sea with it in thy youthful and carefree days?'

'Night ye was born.'

'Again?'

'Last I saw the creature – night ye was born.'

Mine eyes narrowed for my patience were come to its end with this nettlesome old one. She were conjurin things forta ruffle me. She bin sent by the Prelate forta stir trouble, sure and certain.

'Blather-spake!'

'Tis noh, these hands brought ye into the world,' sayt she, raisin her wrinkly old mitts. 'I know ye were born feet first as the Prelate tolt ye.'

'All Grathico knows.'

'Aye, but all Grathico doesnoh know that ye didnoh kill yer mother.'

My hand become tight round the sword.

'Thou art spakin bout things thou shouldst noh – best explican thysen, quick-like.'

'I know cause I were there in the bothy, night ye was born – as were he.'

'The Prelate?'

'Aye.'

'What bothy?'

'The bothy ye now lives.'

'What about it?'

'Tis where ye was born.'

I grabbed her garment where her shrivelly old breasts were hid and put the sword to her throat.

'Blather-spake! Thou knows naught about it. Bin sent by the Prelate with some devilish purpose. Thinkest thou I'm dozy?'

'Wouldst slit the throat of a feeble old mother, wouldst thee?' sayt she, all sneery and scornful.

'Would,' sayt I. 'Will, if she keeps tellin lies.'

'She doesnoh tell lies.'

The crone pulled away then, continuin to move round the havocked body of the whale. I followed, keepin a close eye in case she had more ideas about layin her hands upon it.

'Exquisite creature, ainny?' sayt she, noddin twort the whale.

'Has come forta admire the Fish?'

The crone gathered her dress and crouched aneath Levi's opened belly. Sittin there on her ownsome with her legs curled aneath her she looked like a child, an oldenin wizened child with white hair crouchin afore a great beast. Most the butter-flies had lost interest in the visitor and had settled back upon the flesh of the whale.

'Sit,' sayt she.

I shook the skull.

'Ye need the rest.'

'I'm grand,' sayt I, though truth be tolt I were in no state to be standin for periods on end.

'Ye are noh – sit.'

She tilted her skull when she sayt that, her voice were soothin and she spaked so soft and feminine that I were near inclined to sit. That were the first spell it occurred to me that praps I werenoh spakin with an oldenin Grathica but a spirit of the Wastes. The crone attempted a falterin smile, a peace offerin I spose it were meant to be, but I were on my guard and noh inclined twort smilin. In a sudden, she'd become very comfortable with hersen, the jitters were gone and she seemed at home in the Wastes with mysen and the whale – what unsettled me, truth be tolt.

'Yer mother lived in the bothy ye now lives – it were built by the Prelate forta house her.'

'Blather-spake.'

'She were mute, didst thee know that?' sayt she, payin me no mind. 'Stopped spakin her tenth year. She were quiet any-wise, ner sayin much of aught. Unsettlin it were – her walkin round all silent with the big eyes and the endless black hair trailin her like a weepin veil. She'd be upon ye afore ye knowt it – a pale raven-haired wight, mute and fey. She clammed up round the time the marks appeared on her flesh, thin gashes runnin down the side of her face what seemed to appear over-night. For a spell she were considered a vessel though prone to wild moods wherein she'd suffer fits and convulsions of the body, makin animal sounds in back of her throat as though possessed by the Devil himsen. Her spirit oscillated some – quiet and still one moment, mutinous and unbroken the next.

'When she were about yer age – younger mind – her belly started showin and there were murmurs she'd sneaked out the village and lain with a spirit of the Wastes. It were sayt she'd wandered as a child and had knowt the flesh of the Devil who'd stolen her tongue so as she could tell no soul what bin done upon her. It were sayt that's where the marks upon her skin come from – a keepsake from when she'd lain with the Beast. Prelate says the Devil has a gestation all its own and is born whensoever it wills; it lay dormant inside her, waitin and growin, causin her to have the episodes where she'd shake and quiver so, the growlin what come from inside her were the seed of the Devil blasphemin from the womb. Prelate says it were the Devil's child what kep her voice captive, holdin her tongue inside her with its wee evil and unborn hands.

'After yer mother started showin she were brought afore the congregation; in the house of God, afore all the souls of Grathico, the Prelate tore at her dress so that she had to wrap her arms round hersen to keep it from fallin. The same long thin scars that were upon her face scored the flesh betwix her shoulders. *The mark is upon her,* sayt he. *Her body is knowt to the Beast and she is pregnant with its child.* Afterwards, she had to be ushered away so she werenoh stoned to death right there in the square. The bothy were built soon after and she were removed from Grathico, banished to the Wastes so as her child could be born into the desolation it belonged.'

A butterfly landed upon the crone's leg, causin her to flinch some. Becomin still, she lifted her eyes as though enquizzenin mine opinion on the matter but I werenoh inclined to console her and so pretended noh to notice.

'As midwife I were charged with mindin her,' sayt she, 'bringin her food and makin sure she were in health. It were done in secret a course, though the Prelate ner let me alone with her – allway one of his men were sent to oversee what passed betwix us. She spent her time fussin round the bothy – preparin it for ye. She fashioned the bottom drawer of the cupboard into a crib – placin it near her bed and fillin it with soft things to lay ye upon. She seemed noh to notice I were there mostspells, keepin hersen busy movin things from one side the room to the other, mutterin to hersen in what sounded like a language all its own. Other spells I'd find her standin at the window starin out upon the sea for hours on end, like it had possession of her soul.'

The old woman paused, vain-waitin for me to say somethin but I had naught to say and kep the gob shut.

'The mornin come I found her standin over a puddle on the floor, the insides of her thighs and calves drippin with the fluid what supported ye. I cleaned her and did what I could forta make her comfortable afore runnin back to the village to tell the Prelate. The day were fierce squelchy and the guard what returnt with me were forced to stand outside in the wet so he could be sent forta summon the Prelate when she were closer the time.

'I placed the blanket and things she used for sleepin in the middle of the floor and laid her upon em, but she wouldnoh keep still – no sooner were she down then she'd be up again, pacin across the hut. She kep tryin the handle of the door, lookin at me like I were the Devil himsen for she knowt I had the key tied round my neck. The rain come hard and clamour-some, poundin upon the thin roof above. Stoppin her pacin, she tilted her face to the skies afore turnin to me – beseechin and reproachful – but I kep shakin my head and tried to get her back down upon the blankets. In a sudden, she charged me forta wrest the key from my neck. I didnoh fight agin her for I didnoh want to rouse the attention of the guard. I tried to prevent her from goin outside but she couldnoh be stopped.

'Comin out the door the guard looked upon her as though noh knowin whether he should force her back inside or lower his eyes, but he couldnoh stop from starin, and turnt red at the sight of the wild and silent creature full with child. Yer mother squelched about in the weather, watchin the mud seep betwix her toes. Her black hair – blacker still in the wet – fell across her face in dark clumps and sat plastered agin her skin. Her dress, what soon become soaked and sheer, clung to her exag-

125

gerated form; it clung to the swell of her breasts and belly, to the curve of her back and thighs. The wet sat upon her skin in droplets as the dull grey light of day moved betwix her limbs. Her body become a shadow of swell and wain slitherin inside the swathe of her dress. I mind it well, I mind it clear and without stain – her full with ye, the undulatin feminine shadow of her in the Wastes, feet caked in filth.'

'Whisht!' sayt I. 'Thou art a spirit of the Wastes come forta blandish and beguile me, thou hast come forta lull me into enfeeblement with blather-spake and the like.'

I werenoh accustomed to hear women spaked about in such manner, it werenoh bidden, truth be tolt, and left me dizzy and feverish. Squintin hard at the crone, I could see the duplicitous and knavery spirit movin about inside her oldenin bones. Thing were though, I were none too convicted in tryin to stop her spakin, and she knowt it – what made me angry, sure and certain, mine inability to stop her, even though I knowt I should.

'I watched her from the door a spell, beckonin her inside. When she wouldnoh come I went out to join her. She allowed me to put mine arm under hers and we walked about like that, her hummin strange, absonant tunes – eyes down, squelchin bout in the wet and mud. *Thou wilt be a mother*, I tolt her, *thou shalt become a mother soon*, sayt I, but she kep silent and didnoh lift her eyes. After a longspell I managed to coax her back inside to the warmth of the fire. She were smilin – the heat of the flame and her own devilry amused her, I spose. I sat her down and washed the mud off her feet, what made her laugh like a child, for she werenoh much beyond one hersen. While I were scrubbin the floor, she rose and went to the hearth. Liftin her dress, she tucked it under the weight of her breasts and warmed her belly agin the

126

fire – when that werenoh enough she pulled the dress over her head, droppin it to the ground aside her. I spied the guard peakin through the window, rain drippin from his neb, mist of his breath gatherin agin the glass. She refused to put the dress back on, so I hung it near the fire and fixed a sheet across the window, though I werenoh spose to. She went back to warmin her belly, rubbin it all over in soothin circular motions as I studied the mark of the Beast upon her back, her body flickerin afore the light of the fire.'

The crone rested her pale and wrinkly hands across her middle, rubbin em round and round her own oldenin belly.

'The sun were settin and the dress back on her by the time she were due,' sayt she. 'I'd her lain upon the soft things in the centre of the hut, but she kep pullin em from aneath her, preferrin the hardness of the wood. His dark sen had bin summoned and were stood in the corner of the bothy – the cloak and beak of his vestments flitterin round the edges of mine eyes, makin my hands shake as I tended her.

'She were moanin as the pangs welled and waned, her face misshapen with pain, for I donoh think she knowt what to expect. The Prelate begun to beat his cane agin the floor and recite from the Book. The thuddin were rhythmic and constant, as though a great heart were beatin aneath the floor. Drippin wine on her lips, I smeared the warm goat's blood upon her while recitin the Four Bloods – *Blood on blood in blood – through blood*. It is a chant forta keep the woman centred, the one birthin is spose to say the final *through blood* but that werenoh to be with yer mother, so I sayt it for her.'

The crone turnt to me.

'The goat's blood is to help ease the child through the mother,' explicant she. 'I struggled to keep the birthin sheet on her, for she were movin and wrigglin about so. The wooden heartbeat and the Prelate's footsteps come closer and I could feel the thud of the cane through my hands and knees. Standin over yer mother, he watched the pangs of birth writhe across her face.

'As ye begun yer passage through her, her distress increased and her hand fell out from under the blanket and begun clawin at the wood. I took it in mine so that she'd have somethin to squeeze and ease her pain but the Prelate wouldnoh allow it and swiped at me with his cane.'

Risin to her feet, the crone picked up a large conical shell from the shore and helt it to her neb.

'She isnoh to be touched!' bawled she, conjurin the Prelate.

She made her voice deep, emulatin his own, though it were distorted some from havin the shell pressed agin her mug.

'Yer mother wouldnoh let go but tightened her grip upon me, squeezin my hand till it become sore and smartin with the nails diggin in and drawin blood. *Get her off ye!* sayt he. I become desperate tryin to pull my hand free. The Prelate raised his cane and I throwt mysen across her so as he couldnoh harm her, or ye what were inside. As I lay across her, the birthin seized her body and she wailed in pain – she howled the pangs of birth, soundin the torment of all the years of her long silence.

'The Prelate tolt me to keep her quiet, but I sayt she bin quiet long enough – *Shut her*, sayt he, *or ye'll rot in the Wastes with her!* Placin my fingers upon her lips I stroked her damp face forta calm and quieten her, tellin her it were time to bring forth her child. She seemed to listen to what I sayt her for she forgot all about the Prelate and me, and instead concentrated on movin ye through her body, and soon, lookin betwix her legs I saw yer wee feet had come forth, glistenin with blood and fluid as ye parted her in two.'

The crone looked at me all fairy-eyed then, tendersome praps, till her face changed in a sudden, becomin venomous and twisted.

'*Get the sheet over her! The child comes wanton and back-ward!* sayt he. With ye comin out legs first, I had to reach in with the thumbs and help bring yer wee waist through.'

Crouchin down on her haunches, the crone helt her hands in front of her as though she were deliverin me all over again.

'Yer mother's eyes become an awe-makin colour green from the stress of givin birth and then – next thing I knowt – there ye were with the black hair she bequeathed ye, thrustin yer wee limbs about. First I thought somethin were wrong but ye were just shocked to be outside her and had naught to say for yersen. And that were it, more or less, ye slipped silent-like into the world and I happed ye up in the soft things yer mother'd prepared for ye. She hersen were spent, lathered in sweat and pantin – I mind that too, the sound of her breath and the spit and crackle of the fire as yer silent slithery sen wriggled about in mine arms. The caul what surrounded ye in the womb were still on yer new birthed crown and despite what the Prelate sayt about ye comin breached and ill-starred into the world, I kenned otherwise for it is knowt among midwives, among women, that exitin the womb with the caul part attached is a sign of providence and reckonin – whether it were in weal or woe thou wert a marked child, but noh in the way he thinks.'

She raised her skull to me.

'The men donoh know everythin what happens under these skies – nourished in our bodies they come, wersh and squea-lin we bring em into the world . . .'

But the crone didnoh finish her thought and instead rose to her feet.

'*Go!* he tolt me. *Take the child and return to the village,*' sayt she in the low voice. 'The Prelate were stood over me with the cane and I had no choice but to do as I were tolt. Once outside

129

though I couldnoh leave, so the two of us – I and ye – ducked round the further side of the bothy what faced upon the sea. Peepin through the window I saw him lookin down upon her. She were flushed from birthin – the fluids and placenta what lay spilt betwix her legs glistened aneath the flame of the fire. I could feel the still and quiet inside, till I saw yer mother's lips move and heard the strange lilt of her voice comin through the wall – muffled and faint it were, like a bird aneath a pillow . . .'

Tuckin the shell under her arm, the crone helt out a cupped hand as though an injured bird lay within. Raisin it to her eye she rested her other hand, soft and delicate, upon it.

'The Prelate were still, the glass panel of his eye swathed in the flickerin yellows and ambers of the fire. In a sudden, he reached down and begun tearin at her dress – unresistin his violence, she allowed hersen to be pulled about as though already limp and lifeless. Dress torn from her, she slumped agin the floor, unclad and bare afore him, breasts full with the milk what would clabber and curdle inside her. The Prelate lifted the pitcher of goat's blood and poured it over her breasts and belly, he poured it betwix her legs what made her squirm, for she were still raw from givin birth. Throwin it aside, it smashed agin the wall – blood leached twort the floor, seepin into the grain of the wood. Straddlin her new-birthed and deflated belly, he rubbed the blood into her skin, into her breasts and lips afore restin his hands upon her throat.'

The crone were crouched over, her hand bent into a wrinkly old claw. I imagined her afore me – this woman, my mother, so sayt the crone – lyin in the sand with the gloved hand of the Prelate wrapped round her throat. Her face were all clarty with blood but it were her fingers what helt mine attention –

the way they kep diggin into the sand over and over, makin ruts in it like the paws of an animal.

'Placin her own hand agin the one what were round her throat, yer mother looked into the mask and smiled. I turnt away from the window then,' sayt the crone, 'for it werenoh his violence but her smile I couldnoh endure.'

The old woman become silent, fixin me with a very meaninful look.

'It were then I saw the Leviathan,' sayt she, scourin mine eyes. 'With my back agin the bothy and yer wrigglin newborn sen in mine arms I stared into the comin dark and saw that otherworldly creature launch into the air, arch its back, and thrash itsen agin the surface of the sea. The eventide were so still ye could hear the slap and batter of its great body returnin to the water. Ye cried out at the sight of it, for ye knowt it were there – ye must have sensed it, for it werenoh fortuity or chance. It were near the first sound ye ever made, howlin at that creature, openin yer wee mouth to bawl and halloo for joy at the sight of the Leviathan.

'I clapped my hand across yer mouth and listened to the sound of the Prelate's footsteps approachin the window as ye wriggled and weltered in mine arms. Holdin my breath, I watched his beaked shade spill into the Wastelands and slither across the ground afore us. I were afeared I might suffocate ye or that ye'd cry out again if I took my hand away, so we made a scutter for it, sneakin back round the bothy twort the village. When I knowt it were safe, we turnt round to see the flicker of the fire in the window and the Leviathan mullin round in the shimmery, aqueous dark – head above the surface, blowin its lungs into the stars. We watched till the creature sounded; flukes flickin water at the moon as it righted itsen and sunk into the depths, back into the dark sigh from which it come.'

The crone fell silent then, I had the skull down but I knowt she were lookin upon me.

'Thou art a spirit of the Wastes,' sayt I, quiet-like.

She shook the skull.

'We come back to the village agether and I took ye into my home, as were agreed.'

'I lived with ye?'

'Aye, ye lived with me yer first three years, in the very house what ye had, till recent, come for the food.'

She eyeballed me some, lettin me know mine absence werenoh gone unnoticed.

'I expected him to come for ye daily – to do ye harm, but it took three years, and when he come it were to take ye into his house noh throw ye into the sea, though I spose he'd gotten rid of ye the night ye was born if that were what he intended. We was harried by the souls of the village all those three years. Sacred Stones were left on the porch in the shape of a cross, somespells we'd waken to find a great circle of em layin round the house. The women of the village gathered all hours to sing hymns of purification, we'd be wakened by their shrill voices comin out the dark. The red cross were painted in animal blood upon the door and windows to block the egress of spirits. I spent most those years clutchin ye to my breast, terrified indoors. I were ostracised from the village for housin ye, but souls knowt ye was there by will of the Prelate, so no harm were visited upon us.

'Ye growt accustomed to it, for it were all ye knowt, the women's songs sent ye to sleep like they was cradle songs. Ye played with the Sacred Stones on the porch, makin shapes and structures from em. One night, ye sallied out yer cot and somewise opened the door; standin on the porch ye sung their songs back to em with yer strong child's voice, for ye knowt

132

each word by heart. When I come to bring ye back inside the women was all silent, the whites of their eyes starin out the dark, quiet and awestricken at yer wee sen standin there in nightdress, singin unto em. It were soon after that the Prelate come for ye, sent his men forta gather ye, and that were it, the time of cleansin were over and I were unbidden to spake or approach ye from that day forth – ye were in his house then, and there were naught what could be done about it.'

The crone looked upon me all hangdog and maudlin.

'Mind ye aught of that?'

'I cannoh mind what ner happened, can I?'

Her eyes fell to the sand – despondency itsen. I were reluctant to believe what she sayt for ye couldnoh trust a word what spilt from the gob of a Grathican. The only thing a soul could rely upon were the thoughts in his own skull – and I were suspicious of those too, truth be tolt.

'How dost thou know it is the same creature?'

'*Thou* knows it is the same,' sayt she.

'Thou art a spirit of the Wastes,' I tolt her.

Her eyes sunk, sheepish some or sorrowful.

'Out!' sayt I, pointin the sword upon her. 'Go afore thy wrinkled old gullet be slit.'

She got to her feet quick-like, keepin her orbs upon the shore.

'Blather-spake! Blather-spake and deception!' bawled I, nudgin her with the blade.

Turnin to me, the old woman behelt mine eyes.

'Thou knows otherwise.'

She turnt the back upon me then and I watched her oldenin body march itsen up along the shore. In a distance she stopped and looked down at her side – as though havin just minded it were there, she opened her fist and let the shell fall from her hand.

XV

I lit a fire outside the hollow wherein the yawl were kep so as smoke could escape and flames could warm the rock and dry the sea-drenched blankets I'd draped within. Linin the yawl with some of the warmed and tattered fleece I snuggled in a spell while attemptin to keep one orb on Levi though, truth be tolt, I were half in the land of sloom when a bevy of butterflies entered forta waken me. I brushed em away, bit irritable-like, for I were possessed by a fierce skullache and noh ready to be roused. They was such that when I opened the gob forta yawn, wings would be all inside there, flappin about. The creatures emsens become het-up and indignant, thrashin agin the sides of my mouth – *Let us out of yer disgustin gob, beast-boy! It is wet and dark and unpleasant in here!* I were none too fond of em flutterin round in there neither.

'Geh off,' I tolt em, spittin em from the gob and swipin at em with the hand, but they paid no heed and kep ditherin about my person. 'This is yer doin,' sayt I to Levi as I rose and slipped out the hollow.

Leave em be, sayt she, *thou art in a mood is all.*

I grumbled some under the breath, for it were true I were a slugabed and noh my best sen upon wakin. Stretchin the pegs I picked up the spear and, in a huff, made for the sea so as to splash water on the mug and noh look upon things what lay or fluttered upon the shore, for no matter how much ye may think em awe-makin and astonishin creatures, somespells even whales and butterflies will be a great disappointment unto ye – that stark and troublin revelation come next in *The Philosophy of the Wastelands*.

With the sea still drippin from the mug, I looked out across the water twort a bleary sun raisin its skull over our ragged shores. A voice come to me then, it were in a distance and dwam-makin, and for a wee glorious spell I thought the sun were singin to me till I realised the voice were comin from behind and were very familiar. Turnin round I looked beyond the Great Fish and sure enough atop the cliff stood a cluster of Grathicans.

Front and centre were Withy's tall and gangly sen; standin apart from the others he helt his hands by his side as his rare and gossamery voice rolled round the cliffs as though he were singin in a great amphitheatre and all the sea were his audience. The Closemen were gathered behind him and – though it took a spell for me to understand what it were – I saw a pole had bin erected in the middle of the men from which hung a body, lax and unstirrin. I begun walkin then runnin twort em, butterflies scatterin about me as I went.

What ailes our beast-boy then? sayt they as I come past, a few risin forta follow me.

When I come to the top of the cliff the singin stopped and, in the silence and distance, the men stood lookin upon me. I slipped out the spear I'd secured to the back and stared at em in a kind of flather as to what ado next. Withy moved to the fore and started singin again, starin straight upon me he made a wee sneaky gesture with his hand – it were slight and fleetin and it were hard to know what he meant but I took it to mean *have strength* or *keep the chin up* or somethin of the kind. Upon makin the sign he turnt and wended his way through the others what fell in behind him. Followin his voice they marched back into the bleakness, the sparse quitch what growt there become crushed aneath their heavy cloaks as they disappeared over the rocks, guided and protected through the Wastes by his song.

The pole had bin wedged betwix rocks with other stones placed and piled round the base forta keep it steady while the body fettered to it hung slack and wilted. The skull were slumped fort with the long grey hair hangin loose across the mug. Her feet were bare and her legs part exposed. The rope what bound her cut into and blackened her skin. The teeth marks of the imps were on all parts of her flesh, they were upon her arms and fingers and the sliver of gullet what could be seen betwix her hair. They'd even taken to her lugs – bloody holes and tears at the tips what looked as though a small dog had chewed there. Her dress were perforated, blotched red all over from where the imps' teeth had sunk into her flesh.

With the tip of the spear, I swept the hair from her mug.

'Kaaaaaahhhhh,' sayt she, takin a lungful of air as she raised her skull and opened two festerin orbs.

I were startled at the dereliction of the crone's face and the fact of her still breathin sen. The imps had devoured her

136

features, their mark were upon her neb and lips, the long thin scrapin of their teeth ran down her brow and temple. Two thin crimson lines ran from the corners of her engorged eyes sluicin their way down her cheeks in unbroken wee streams of bloody tears. Swingin her skull back-a-fort, she searched for me through the dark.

'Thou, is it?'

'Aye,' sayt I.

There come a wee fragile curlin at the edges of her gob.

'I didnoh take the blessin,' sayt she, as though she were a bold child.

'Nay, ye didnoh.'

'Devil took my sight, then the imps come peckin and bitin my flesh, I were brought through the Wastes till Melas come loud and close. Death sung to me all the while, but I waited ye, I blocked the ears and waited ye to come.'

There were a fervour in her voice, as though the desecration of her body had sent her mind knarry and frail. Her raw, inflamed eyes moved about vain and unprofitable in her skull.

'Thou wilt enfold me?' enquizzened she. 'Afterwards, thou wilt bury me?'

'Aye.'

'Thou shalt perform the ablutions and prepare this body for His gracious hands. Thou shalt wash and lay to rest these old bones – this spent flesh.'

'Aye,' sayt I, 'I will.'

I come close, raisin the spear and weavin it through the rope to where I thought her heart lay. She took hold of the shaft and adjusted it some.

'There,' sayt she.

137

As I looked into the gnarled and pitiful mug of the old woman her hands come free of the spear. Holdin em palm out, her bloody gaze searched for me but instead fixed upon a void above my skull.

'When yer mother were afore the fire, dryin her engorged flesh, heavy and abundant with ye . . .'

The old woman begun movin her hands about, wrigglin her fingers as though massagin an invisible thing afore her.

'. . . I allway imagined yer wee unborn hands inside her, warmin emsens agin the linin of her belly.'

The spear come away when she sayt that, for her words had shaken my resolve. Feelin the point leave her chest, the orbs become lively and sore-lookin in her skull. A smile gathered at the corners of her mouth as though behind the ruin of her face she were very pleased with hersen.

'I allway knowt we would be reconciled. Thou minds the old woman what raised ye.'

Such were the last words formed by her ancient lips afore her skull slumped fort and she were taken into the spirit world.

I stood a spell, mesmerised by the hellish gape of the old woman's orbs as they stared down upon me from aneath the veil of brittle smoky hair. Clamberin up the stones, I tried to unbind her, but the rope were impossible to untie and so I come behind the pole and begun jabbin at it with the spearhead forta unfetter her thatwise. After cuttin through the third or fourth windin, the rope become loose and the old woman fell fort in a sudden, tumblin into the Wastes – *Thoooff!* sayt she, as her body plummeted to the ground.

I become still and mortified.

'Sorry, mother,' hushpered I. 'Sorry there.'

I dragged her body to the edge of the cliff so as she were nearer the sea. Runnin back down the shore I collected water to wash her body. Crouchin over her, I bathed her wrinkled old skin in the dark and gelid brine. Washin her feet and hands in silence, I rested her skull in one hand and poured water upon her hair, baptisin her into the ceaseless shade of the lowlands. I arranged and put to rest her silent soul upon the ground; I straightened her legs and placed her arms by her side, palms flat agin the unconsecrated soil of the Wastes. Clusterin rocks forta place upon her body, I spied somethin glisterin in the sun. Half concealed by the sparse and wispy branches of a shrub, a tool of sorts lay nestled in the dust. The instrument looked like tongs cep with sharp pincers either side, all four covered in blood what were also smeared across the helve.

Comin back to the old mother, I placed the tool agin her and saw it matched the incisions in her body – the teeth marks the imps had left in her skin. In the skull I saw noh the spirits of the Wastelands but the instruments of man gougin into her flesh as she howled from within the unlit Hell of her blinded and bloody orbs. Suppressin the fury boilin in the bones, I saw to the old woman, makin sure she were ended proper. I were meticulous in placin the stones upon her, for it seemed of great importance, as though it were helpin to arrange and order the rage what burrowed inside me. I sat with her a longspell, imaginin her old and frail sen in the darkness as the stones lay heavy upon her, coaxin her into the earth. Her orbs were closed and covered, the smooth damp stone lay across her mouth – Mortality's cold finger pressin agin her lips, hushin her into eternity.

XVI

Marchin back to Levi I prepared mysen for war. Takin hold of the sword I cut a great flap of blubber from her flank. Makin a hole in the middle I slipped it over the skull so that two slabs of flesh hung down my back and chest – a habergeon of whale flesh it were. I cut a length of rope from the pulleys and, usin it as a girdle, drew the blubber round my waist forta keep her close agin me. Plungin the blade inside her I withdrew the last of her blood. Dippin my fingers into the red viscousness I smeared it across my cheeks and forehead where it soon dried and cracked agin the skin. Facin Levi I breathed in deep, enjoyin the stench of her flesh upon me.

Thou art leavin me? enquizzened she.

'For a spell,' sayt I.

I allway knowt this day would come, still-yet, I am noh prepared.

'I shall bring thee somethin upon my return.'

Thoust better, sayt she, *or ye'd neednoh bother comin back at all.*

I took off then, headin up the sand twort Grathico with the butterflies risin behind me like a storm fermentin in the heavens. Sweepin into the sky they crackled and kitter-kattered and so fort, chargin the air with static and fervour. I come to life feelin em swarm and hum behind me; they sent shivers up-a-down the spine and filled me with fierce grit and purpose. Fettled in the flesh of the Leviathan I marched upon Grathico – hook in one hand, sword in the other, a plague of butterflies forta serve as mine army.

I followed the shoreline to the cliff what rose behind Grathico, for it were mine intention to approach from that direction rather-en cut through the Wastes. The butterflies growt fluttersome and anxious waitin for my slow and human sen to ascend the rocks.

'I werenoh born with wings, lads!' hallooed I upon em.

Once I were nearin the top of the cliff I stopped and spaked low and hushpery.

'Ye each stay here,' I tolt em. 'There'll be no creepin upon naught with ye gaggle of glisterin articles flutterin about the place.'

But truth is they was already stopped there, hoverin just aneath the lip of the cliff, wherefore I were forced to climb through a great cloud of quiverin wings which, as ye may expect, is noh an easy thing ado, especial considerin I were concentratin hard upon where next to put the feet. Some-spells I used the hook forta grab hold of the rock and haul mysen up thatwise. When I come over the cliff face and started out for the village, a single butterfly separated from the others forta follow me.

'Thy wings are fierce gaudy,' sayt I, tryin to be delicate about it, but it seemed to matter naught to the creature what flew straight by me without a word. 'OK,' sayt I, 'but try noh to flutter so, thou willst bring unwanted attention to thysen – and mysen and all.'

The butterfly took no notice of that advice neither and fluttered about like a drunken mooncalf. Mostspells it looked as though it were about to fall from the sky all agether, then at the last moment it would lift itsen, jitterin bout all higgledy-piggledy.

'Thou art noh very good at that, art thou?' sayt I.

Grathico were soon afore me. It bin a longspell since I'd looked upon the village from that aspect, I'd forgotted how green it were, how kep and mannered it seemed. It were sheer quaint and all, what with the smoke leachin from the chimneys that spiked its wee skyline. From a distance it did look like God's country, cep the smell praps, the faint waft of rotted birds and bonemeal.

I stood afore the Fens, the very same I use to prowl with Withy back in the weantime when he'd taken me about as my guardian. To prowl the Fens meant protect the limits of Grathico, it didnoh mean enterin em but skirtin em close. Grathicans werenoh permitted inside the Fens, for although they werenoh the Wastes proper they was still hostile and injurious to God-fearin souls. The Fens were a purgatory what engirdled Grathico, they were an inbetwix place where the blessed and blighted converged, where both were diluted and fortified to become another thing all agether. It were sayt that within their limits coexisted ineffable sufferin and joy, and that such conflict, if entered upon, would tear the soul apart.

The weans clustered to play games there; collectin creatures, they'd throw em over the limits of Grathico then entice em back with scraps of food afore clobberin em with rocks or cudgels, killin the polluted animals as they tried to return to consecrated ground. Sundry wee and bloody battlefields sprung up at different points along the borderlands, swathes of earth bespattered with the corpses of mice and rats or somespells birds and the goats what roamed the Wilds, all lured to their deaths by the yennin in their bellies and the violence of the weans – brained and bleedin, their bodies lay stretched across the bloodslaked verges, dividin the sacred and profane.

It werenoh far from here, when I were but a wean mysen, that I first come to realise I were part beast, part boy. I mind it well, for I were tryin to act the big man by tellin Withy how when I got old enough I were goin to capture a spirit of the Wastes.

'That right?' enquizzened he.

'Aye.'

'With what?'

'Again?'

'I'm curious to know with what ye intend to hunt spirits of the Wastes.'

I took a spell to think upon it.

'A spear!' bawled I, raisin the arm like there were a spear in it.

'Thou hast no spear.'

'I'll make one, I'll make a spear with mine own hands.'

'I donoh think spirits of the Wastes are too nettled about spears, even ones made by thine own hands.'

'What does one use to dispose em good and proper then?'

'A Spirit Catcher,' sayt he.

143

'What's that?'

'A thing what catches spirits.'

'How does it look, this Spirit Catcher?' enquizzened I, noh aware he were makin fun of me, for I took my spirits very serious back in the weantime, still do mostspells.

'A Spirit Catcher is made from a cage what has bin blessed and inside ye must place soil from the Wastes, upon which ye lay the heart of a wee innocent boy from Grathico,' sayt he, lookin very intent upon me. 'Like yesen, for example.'

I stopped and stared upon him.

'That's noh true.'

'Is it noh?' sayt he with the eyebrow arched, lookin straight into mine orbs – what gave me the qualms, truth be tolt.

'Is it?' enquizzened I.

He didnoh respond but turnt and walked on.

'Is it, Withy?!'

Traipsin after him, I become quiet and broody.

'I reckon ye could catch a spirit without usin a real boy heart,' sayt I.

'How's that?'

'Well, I imagine the spirits' brains have turnt to mush from bein in the Wastes so long that ye could use a goat heart instead – I bet they wouldnoh tell the difference.'

'Goat heart taste different to boy heart, a spirit of the Wastes knows better-an any soul.'

'He willnoh know till he is inside the Spirit Catcher and then it'll be too late!' sayt I, very cock-a-hoop and triumphant.

'Maybe,' sayt Withy, a smirk upon his mug, 'maybe.'

Somethin caught mine attention then, a small creature dartin twort the Fens.

'An imp!' screeched I. 'An imp of the Wastes!'

I took after the creature, Withy laughin behind me.

'Scat sprite! Out ye wee desolate spirit of the Wilds. Out!' sayt I, boundin down the slope.

I were goin to drive the imp back to the Wastes or if it wouldnoh leave I would wring its neck for havin trespassed upon Grathico. A brave soul I were as a wean, herdin the Devil back into the Wilds.

I were runnin fast as the pegs would carry me, leppin and boundin through the wheat fields with all my concentration upon the imp what darted this-way-a-that.

'Yaaaa! Yaaaa!'

I chased him a longspell for he were a quick and slippery sprite what seemed intent upon tauntin me. Stoppin every-now-a-then, he turnt the skull – *What's all the hallooin for then?* sayt he, afore scutterin off again. In the end he got away a course, boundin down a steep incline what I couldnoh follow. Turnt out it were only a hare – I think I knowt it were a hare the wholespell but mine imagination had gone wild and so I'd convinced mysen it were an imp, for I needed to chase some-thin and expel the energy. It were only then, as I were slouched over catchin the breath and watchin the hare disappear, that I become aware of Withy bawlin and hallooin upon me.

Way in a distance at the edge of the wheat fields, Withy were stood with his hands upon his head. He were silent as I looked upon him and mine expression become squishy and furrowed wonderin what all the bother were about. Takin one hand from the skull he pointed to the ground. It come to me slowise like my body understood afore my skull. Lookin aneath me I felt the fear pass through my feet and climb my pegs, floodin my chest so as I couldnoh breath. When I lifted the skull to look upon Withy he had come to his knees.

Without knowin it, I'd run clear through the Fens and crossed into the Wastelands.

Apart from the large wooden gate with the bony cormorant wings stretched and nailed upon it there was no walls round Grathico – a double line of Sacred Stones was all what separated the God-fearin from the godless. All Grathicans knowt it from the womb; blindfolded we knowt – by instinct, habit, and above all fear – where God's mercy ended.

I stood there a longspell, noh able to think or do aught cep let the waves of terror wash over me. I become frozen to the spot as though the ground aneath had sprouted hands what had grabbed hold of mine ankles. Lookin upon the feet, I waited for em to catch fire or for the earth to open up and swallow me whole. A warmth spread betwix the legs as a dark patch formed upon the breeches – I imagined it were my soul leavin me, my spirit were bein taken from me and dragged into the Netherworlds. Withy calt to me again; I couldnoh understand what he sayt but I lifted the skull and started runnin. I ran back through the Fens and into the fields, I ran past Withy who stepped away from me as I come past – gob open, he stared upon me like he seen the Devil himsen. I ran back to the village and hid under the Prelate's house where the firewood were kep, and there I lay tryin to cleanse mysen in the consecrated ground of Grathico. Aneath the blessed house of the Prelate I rolled in the dirt and rubbed it into my skin, I sayt every prayer imaginable and cursed mysen to Hell. After a longspell I heard the Prelate's feet cross the porch, come down the steps, and leave through the gate. Slidin from under the house I sneaked inside and climbed straight into bed. Bitin and bawlin into the pillow I threshed my skull agin the mattress and awaited mine own expiry – for the great searin agony

146

of mortality to visit me. I helt my middle for it were writhin and nauseous, and I begun to feel my soul burnin away in the pit of the belly – *That's it, sure and certain*, thought I, *that is the fiery breath of Hell ignitin within me, it shall burn a hole right through my gizzards.* There were tears snakin down the cheeks what I kep wipin with the back of my hand forta see if the blood had yet started to come from mine eyes.

I lay in bed for days for I'd brought a fever upon mysen. I had the sweats and were mumblin about damnation, bletherin gibberish about Spirit Catchers and a hare what had taken my soul and dragged it into the Wastelands. The Prelate come once or twice – sayt I'd bin idlin near the Fens again and had a dose of the Wastes from havin gone too close, sayt it were mine own fault and were only what could be expected from the misbegotted and unobedient. I mind Withy visitin too, skulkin round the door, noh wantin to come near. After days, I begun to sup the soup brought me by the old mother of the house, and slowise I become better – the hallucinations went and I knowt my soul wouldnoh burn in the fiery pits of Hell. Sittin up in bed I stared out at the Wastelands and Melas beyond – contemplatin the unknowt and unbidden what had begun to ferment and simmer inside me. I begun to feel like a wee sorcerer, like somewise I'd brought part of the Wastes back with me. Sittin in the bed my skin brailed as I felt that new and dank world circlin about me, like I could touch it with my hands and pass it round my skull. I were still afeared of the Wastes and all and, in sooth, it were years afore I'd step inside them again without the blessin. Still-yet, it were then, sittin in that bed starin out the window, that I begun to think that praps my kin lay elsewhere and werenoh bound to the limits of Grathico. It were then, as a wee apprentice beast-boy, that I had my first inklin or presentment of Levi and other inbetwix and unworldly things – creatures, spirits, shadows, dust, they was my kin.

I tried to spake to Withy upon it, enquizzenin if he thought everythin the Prelate sayt about the Wastes were true. He looked upon me as though I were a very naive bairn in the woods and, short and curt-like, he tolt me it were true cause the Prelate sayt it were. Withy sayt that all worlds had their limits which were decided upon by those what live within em. He tolt me there were no truth outside man and his God. He sayt that truth werenoh conjured from the air but forged by force and will.

I gave him a look what tolt him I werenoh convinced.

'Truth,' sayt he, 'is a decision.'

He turnt from me then and we ner spaked upon it again. Withy ner tolt another soul about me runnin into the Wastes but things were changed betwix us – from then on I found him lookin upon me slantwise every-now-a-then, watchin to see if he could spy the desolate spirit what lay inside.

Anywise, that were all long ago and things were different now. This spell, as I stood ponderin the Fens with the lone butterfly flappin bout the shoulder, it werenoh the Wastes but Grathico I were trespassin upon – this spell, I were movin from the unconsecrated to the consecrated. Comin through the fields, the wheat were bendin and partin in waves what spread out in a V either side of me. It were just the wind a course, but I felt like the Wastes had come with me, as though its murky spirits had left the shade forta march alongside me. I could see the Prelate's house – the house in where I'd growt – smoke risin from its chimney. He'd noh be able to see me comin from this angle, I knowt that from the many spells I'd sneaked round and back as a wean. It were true I may have bin seen by any soul tendin the fields or walkin betwix the bothies but, truth be tolt, I no longer much cared about bein seen. Calm and slow, the butterfly and I walked through the fields – wheat brushin agin my waist, rappin its wee golden fists upon the flesh of the Leviathan.

XVII

Comin to the Prelate's house, I sneaked upon the porch – the butterfly stayed close, settlin upon my shoulder as I crouched at the window to peep inside. The Prelate himsen were stood with his back to me on the further side of the room, gawpin upon the fields what rolled out to Quag's end and the sea beyond. He were dressed in full garb, cep the cane and mask what lay upon the table. He looked fierce pondersome, truth be tolt, standin there starin into the great unknowt, his long dark frame stark agin the unendin skies what stretched cold and blue across our lonesome ait. It seemed he were waitin upon somethin, I thought praps he were expectin me, praps he were waitin for a certain beast-boy to rise over those hillocks and come for him thatwise – death itsen, comin forta march its shade-makin feet upon Grathico.

The butterfly sallied from my shoulder and come to rest upon the porch. Pausin a spell, it stared at the threshold of the house afore marchin itsen, upon very spindly pegs, twort the gap aneath the door. As it were flutterin the wings and tryin to squeeze through, I lunged forta stop it but were late a course and it disappeared inside. Comin back to the window, I squished the neb agin the glass and waited for the butterfly to show itsen – *What devilry art thou up to?* thought I. Teeterin into view, it stopped to stretch its wings afore flutterin across the room. His dark sen seemin noh to notice as the creature landed on his hand and stared out the window with him – *That there is a handsome view of the Quag in all its glory*, it were thinkin as it sat contemplatin the wonders of nature. Facin the Prelate, it appeared as though the butterfly hushpered somethin soft into his ear, for slowise, he turnt his oldenin and unmasked skull twort it.

It took a spell for the Prelate to register what were in front of him afore he tore his hand away and begun shakin it about like a mooncalf. Spinnin round, he turnt to see me spring like a jack-a-the-box from aneath the window opposite – smilin some, I waved upon him. He didnoh wave back a course, but moved forta block and bar the door, still-yet I were too quick for his oldenin bones and had kicked the door open afore he could prevent it. As I spilt into the room he become doubled over. His gizzards were all at sea, tryin to leap from his gullet on account of the unbearable rot I'd brought into his house. Comin agin the table he reached for the mask what carried the perfumes forta purify the air and protect him from pestilence and disease. Securin it on the skull he stood agin the wall and looked good and proper upon the thing what had entered his house – me a course, a fierce wild beast-boy in all his splendour, blood slathered across the mug, happed up snug and cosy in the flesh of the Leviathan.

'Howbe?' enquizzened I.

Afore he could say aught, the sky begun to darken and there come hallooin and bawlin in a distance. Rushin past me, the Prelate pressed himsen agin the window to peer into the street while I locked the doors either side of the room and slipped the keys sneaky-like into the pocket.

'They wanted to visit as well,' sayt I, squeezin in aside him.

Above the Quag a great smear of butterflies were swarmin in a long meanderin chain across the sky.

'Didnoh trust I were in safe hands, I expect. Couldnoh blame em, all things considered.'

The bawlin growt louder and Grathicans soon come scamperin and scatterin through the streets. Dartin this-way-a-that most ran past the house while others stopped and walked twort it, their mugs becomin pale and slack-jawed when they spied mysen and the Prelate starin out the window. I waved to em as well, for it shall noh be sayt when I wriggle from this mortal and treacherous coil that I werenoh a civilised and well-mannered beast-child of the Wastes – and should ye noh want to take my word upon it, ye'll find that true and undeniable fact inscribed for all eternity into *The Philosophy of the Wastelands*.

Anywise, the Grathicans' opened gobs and wide orbs become skyward and afeared as they spied the butterflies movin upon em. Followin their gaze the Prelate come fort, clangin his beak agin the glass as he tried to peep further into the sky.

'Thy great and cumbersome neb is in the way,' sayt I.

A butterfly flew into the glass with a wallop, causin the Prelate to blanch with the fright. Soon another come, then another, like wee birds they were, beatin soft and blind agin the window. They come sparse at first, then agether in a rush – *kush – kush –*

152

kush – kush – kush – kush, kush, kush! Hearin em agin the walls and the roof, the Prelate cast his beak to the ceilin afore turnin to look upon the window behind – butterflies were gatherin there as well, inchmeal they begun blockin the window panes and trappin the dark inside.

I watched the wee terrified faces of the Grathicans; eyes hollowed and fretful as they flailed the limbs about attemptin to scatter the creatures what tormented em. Some were curled upon the ground like bairns – heads buried in hands they bawled and wriggled about. The Closemen were there a course, still and unmovin midst the melee, the warm plume of their breath disgorgin from their lungs like spirits slitherin from the flesh. Weavin through the bodies and the butterflies come the Stone Thrower; all a flather he were, with the mug flushed and clammy. Stoppin aside the Closemen he stood pantin and threshin the arms about tryin to swipe the creatures from the air, till he spotted me that is, whereupon his face become twisted and the wee gob opened to shout and roar upon my very unwelcomed presence among the charitable and goodly souls of Grathico. I couldnoh hear him a course, what with the clamour outside and the walls inbetwix – still though, I could see the gob open with the squall comin from his lungs. He made a run twort me – forta tear the limbs from my body, I expect – though his plan were thwarted by a Closeman what grabbed hold of his collar. The Stone Thrower were kep from interferin for the house were smottled with butterflies – the souls of the dead as Grathicans saw it, and this were a hallowed conflict overseen by ancient and eternal forces what couldnoh be hindered or violated upon by man. Anywise, with the Stone Thrower frothin at the gob and wrigglin in the arms of the soul what helt him, the Closemen and all Grathicans stood gawkin upon the hooked mask of the Prelate and mine own pale and gory mug as we receded behind the window – enshadowed by our breath upon the glass and the wall of wings what enclosed us.

The Prelate scurried away and I soon heard rattlin behind me.

'Locked,' sayt I, holdin up the keys while peerin, very intent-like, out the window.

Thing were though, I werenoh concentratin on what were goin on outside but more what were happenin behind me, like orbs had growt in the back of my skull – developin strange and mysterious powers I were, as is only right and proper, if ye think upon it, for a beast-boy wrapped in whale flesh. Imaginin his very quavery sen twistin knobs in a flather, a wee devilish smirk curled across my mug, till I heard the cane bein lifted from the table and turnt round to face him.

The room were become dark and quiet cep the flicker of the fire and the vast pot of water boilin atop it. The melee outside sounded distant – a faint, somewise soothin murmur happenin a ways away on a far off ait what had naught ado with me. Wings lifted from the windows, allowin slithers of light to dart across the room and cast different shapes and shadows inside – a wing etched into the wall, the outline of a butterfly turnin or the slash of an antenna cleavin the beaked mask in two. Heat gathered in the house, the glass panels of the Prelate's mask clouded over and it were from inbetwix streaks of condensation that his blue and watery orbs squinted out at me, scornful and repelled. I begun lickin the dry swelter of the room, lappin at it like a creature what senses its surroundins with its tongue.

'Canst thee taste it?'

The Prelate kep the eyes upon me but made no reply.

'Tis caustic and bitter.'

I sniffed upon the air with the neb raised like a dog.

'Smell it too, canst thee? Sulphury, the makin of hellfire and lightnin – that is what ye taught me, is it noh?'

Naught sayt he.

'I've begun to notice a pattern has started to emerge, where-upon souls, by and large, seem very reluctant to spake to me. Hast thou noticed? Praps it is all in my skull?'

When still there were no reply, I lurched fort and wrenched the mask from atop the Prelate's scraggly dome. He swiped and swatted at it like a child but the stench kep him at a distance. Makin a show, I brought the mask level with mine orbs and turnt to face it.

'Praps ye didnoh hear,' sayt I to the mask, raisin my voice as though it were deaf. 'I enquizzened whether or noh thou canst smell it too?'

'What dost thee smell, boy?' sayt I, jigglin the mask up-a-down.

I sniffed the air some so as to make sure my fierce sensitive neb werenoh deceivin me – it werenoh.

'The stench of violence – of savagery long awaited and fore-stalled. Ferity sir, what bin soaked and simmerin in the soul a long longspell.'

'That so?' enquizzened the mask, hangin upon mine every word – curiosity itsen, so it were.

'That's why ye have taken up the cane, is it noh?'

The mask moved back some, mortally offended at the suggestion.

'I've taken up the cane cause a madman, caked in filth and wrapped in the flesh of the Devil, stands afore me.'

155

'A madman?!' sayt I, lookin over my shoulder as though the crackerpot were standin behind me. 'I saw no such thing when I come in – musta scared him off, I expect.'

'Thankye, boy,' sayt the mask, 'thou art a brave and fearless soul.'

'Twere naught, sir, no need to thank me – that thou art safe and snug is its own reward.'

Lettin the mask fall to my side I turnt to look upon the deathly features of his exposed and holy sen – the only signs of life were his orbs, hoverin bright and blue amidst the dull moon of his mug.

'Thou art mad,' sayt he.

And that, my patient and long-sufferin brothers, were the true voice of the Prelate.

'He spakes,' huspered I. 'What meanin has madness in a place such as this?'

As I come fort, he turnt his skull and stumbled backwise tryin to escape the stench. Stalkin the Prelate round the room I tormented him with the reek of whale as he spattered and carried on like a mooncalf. He kep scutterin away, tryin to shirk the miasma of the beast but it were impossible, for the swelter of the room had made it more potent still. Stumblin agin the wall he reached forta open a window but I come fort with the sword to stop him. Unable to hold it further he took a large breath, drawin the stench of the Leviathan deep inside his lungs.

'There ye go,' sayt I, 'lung full of pestilence – yer insides blackenin and rottin as we spake.'

He couldnoh control the wretchin of his gut and, havin nowhere else to go, he emptied his belly upon the floor. Still doubled over he lifted his orbs, starin upon the whale habergeon I wore and the parasites what crawled through its flesh. Gaggin like a thing possessed he turnt away and tried again to rid his belly of the plague.

'Thou shouldst noh have done that upon the Leviathan and her calf – an ungodly, unspakable act.'

Wipin the muck and gack from his gob, he begun quotin from the Book.

'*Thou didst break the sea in pieces by Thy strength. Thou didst shatter the heads of the sea-monsters in the waters. Thou didst crush the head of Leviathan; Thou gavest him to be food to the folk inhabiting the wilderness.*'

'Dost thou noh have a tongue of thine own?'

'My tongue is the Word, they are the same. Return thee to thy wilderness, keep thy shade from Grathico, stain not holy and consecrated ground with thy canker. Feed upon thine own kind – let the flesh of the Beast sustain thee and when thou art worthy I shall come for thee.'

'I'm here now and more-an worthy of thee – thou art afeared and fretful is all, thou wants me gone so as thy pegs may stop quiverin.'

'Fool!'

I moved twort him but he slid across the wall to avoid me.

'Think hard upon how thou addresses me,' sayt I.

The Prelate raised his skull, narrowin the orbs some.

'Ye are in my house, thou does not give orders here, so thinkest thee hard upon how thou addresses me and wary be thy tongue. Sure as the Quag rises from the dark of the sea mine authority upon this ait is absolute, so it has been ordained by God and kin, by holy mandate and blood. To profane and defy me is to defy divine order, it is to do the Devil's work. So thinkest hard, thee, for thou knows naught of

157

the sacrifices made to forge God upon this isle. I, not ye, was there when the anchors were dredged from the crumbling soil and the ships were carried through the desert in search of the sea – the waters having begun to retreat from the shores of Ereb, evaporating afore chastisement and hellfire.'

'I have heard all this afore.'

'And ye shall hear it again, afore ye trespass against me, afore ye trespass against the will of God. It was I, not ye, that marched sixty days and sixty nights as man and beast fell lifeless about me. From the deck of the ship, I watched the fires of the dead consume Ereb. It was I, as a wean and child, who listened to the sound of the souls of the damned being extinguished as they leapt into the sea. So, long and hard may ye think upon how thou addresses me, for there is no sound on God's earth to compare to that of a soul entering Hell.

'This is my house and it is sanctified by God Himsen, its foundations were laid by mine own young and bloody hands – mine and my kin about me. Our blood lies in these walls, it is in the rock and soil that supports them and neither life nor death shall exhume us from this land. Consider well how thou addresses me for I am divine will upon this ait, I am liege over the souls who inhabit it. Ordained by God I stand in this house, so thinkest thee instead by what name I am called, for in these walls, upon this rock, I am the Almighty made flesh and blood.'

I had the skull turnt from him starin upon the fire flickerin in the stove.

'Has God ordained the murder of a mother as she lay in the fluids what sustained her child?' enquizzened I, very calm and quiet. 'It is sayt ye kilt a woman as she lay upon the ground – out there, in the bothy, at the edge of the Wastes.'

158

The lucent orbs shifted some.

'Levi has tolt it me. The Leviathan hersen hushpered it me, for she saw what ye done, she were witness to thy murder.'

'Devil-spake,' sayt he.

'Ordained by God?! Praps it is the fairies what leap through the fields by which thou hast bin ordained, hast thou noh thought of that? Thou hast forgotted em I expect, for they go for allway unsung and unpraised.'

'And what of thy creature?' enquizzened he.

'What about her?'

'What is she but another idol to worship – sheathed in the skin of the Beast thou stands, a heathen from the Wilds, ordained and anointed by a new and false God.'

'God?' enquizzened I. 'A word that cleaves the tongue, in it lurks more terror than the Devil can ferment in all the cauldrons of Hell, for what is more diabolical than the maker of man? What charlatan conjured thee? From the bowels of what atrocity hast thou bin dredged? Brave and divine soul as thou art – murderer of women as they lie upon the ground steeped in the fluids of birth.'

'Whore, not a woman,' sayt he. 'Devil, not a child.'

My skull become light when he sayt that – mine ears went muzzy like they'd noh heard right.

'Again?' enquizzened I.

Tiltin the skull, he behelt mine eyes.

'Whore not a woman, devil not a child.'

I lunged at him then, knockin him down with the helve of the sword.

'What didst thou say?!'

He answered me none, but stayed low and scurried the old-enin bones agin the wall.

159

'Turn around, snake! Come off thy belly!'

But he wouldnoh do as he were tolt.

'Off thy belly snake or I shall be forced to bring thee off mysen! Tell again what thou hast sayt!'

Liftin the skull, the eyes settled upon me, defiant and proud.

'Whore and dev—'

I walloped him afore he had a chance to finish – good and proper I brought my boot upon his skull and he become limp and unconscious.

XVIII

While he were asleep I took hold of his arm and dragged him across the floor; placin a chair afore the window I attempted to lift his heavy and cumbersome sen upon it.

'Up-a-daisy,' sayt I as he grumbled and groaned from deep within the land of sloom.

Bindin his arms behind the chair, I watched the light and shade of the butterflies dance upon his very limp and some-wise peaceful sen. Sittin opposite him I waited, content and cosy in the swelterin heat of the room, strange as that may seem to ye. I were cock-a-hoop, though noh for the reasons ye may think. I liked that everythin had stopped in a sudden, that the Prelate were silent and I were become still. Things had paused and there were naught ado cep listen to the crackle of burnin wood and watch the movement of light and shade slide across the Prelate's slumberin chest. For a spell it felt like I'd slipped into a fissure where the world ceased spinnin and I'd bin given a reprieve – from what I couldnoh say, from everythin I spose, the whole tired lot. For the world ner stops, much as ye may want it to, much as ye may long for rest. It were peaceful and soothin sittin there in the warmth, and I willed things to stay like that, frozen in time, so a spake, with naught ado cep rest and think and breathe.

That's one thing I'd change, if it were up to me, which it's noh a course – I'd make it so the world had to stop every-now-a-then, so as souls could pause a spell and catch their breath, take a nap and wake rested and prepared forta march back into the fray. If it were up to me ye'd get the fiercest sleep ye ever knowt and noh have to wake till ye wanted – a year or two if ye were fierce tired and in much need of rest. Ye'd wake fresh as a daisy, stretchin the wee arms and gob like a new-birthed bairn. That's what I'd do, if it were up to me, which it's noh a course.

Though, truth is, the longer I have ado somethin, the longer I spend starin off into the great abyss, contempla-tin my toes and the many injustices what bin done agin em, or some such haver and trifle. In sooth, it wouldnoh matter how much time or rest I were given, I'd still want more – or think I did anywise. Truth is, there is no solu-tion for the likes of me, there is naught what can be done, so no point wishin for nonsense what cannoh be. That is the conclusion I have come to in my short and illustrious career as a misbegotted though somewhat charmin beast-boy. Still-yet, in all honesthood, I've ner much wanted a solution, I've ner much wanted to be fixed, for it is the bro-ken lonesome parts of the soul what make most sense to me and of which ye should be most proud, those parts what cannoh be touched or knowt – even to thysen, if that make

162

any nous. It is the unknowt what sustains a soul, it is the concealed and untolt what keeps him alife. For a beast-boy without a Wilds to wander through or an endless dark and churnsome sea to ponder is a sad and lonesome thing; a beast-boy without a Leviathan is adrift in the world without purpose – that, as ye may expect, come next in *The Philosophy of the Wastelands*.

I were fingerin the mask, starin upon it and twirlin it in the hands, when the Prelate shifted-some. His garms had become damp with perspiration, his hair fell about his skull in wet clumps. I were perspirin mysen – claggy and stiflin as it were on account of the stove and the butterflies what were wrapped round the house, entrappin the heat. Twitchin some, the skull rose and the Prelate's bleary orbs fixed upon me.

'Hell has come north,' hushpered I.

He winced – wakin to the pain what smarted through his body.

'Leviathan has returnt, she has brought all thy woes upon the shore – the sea has spewed fort great vengeance and reckonin upon thee.'

'Your beast is rotting in the sand,' sayt he, 'like your mother rotted in the sea.'

The blood become cool when he sayt that but I remained composed and unnettled.

'She has kep the waters fierce,' sayt I, 'it is her body inside what torments thee.'

He didnoh like that much and become agitation itsen.

'Ye will beg to be lowered from the pole, drawn and quartered, thou wilt be!'

'Best worry bout thysen,' sayt I, 'all things considered.'

He narrowed the orbs very intent-like.

163

'If ye knew the truth,' sayt he, slack-jawed and droolin, 'ye would not do this thing.'

Leppin from the chair, I raised the sword to his eye but instead of drivin the metal through his skull I snuggled right up close to his lug so as the lips were near pressed agin it.

'I knowt the truth for allway, snake!' hushpered I, hissin and spittin into his hole as he tried to pull away. 'Every soul on this ait knows and thou knows they do thysen! Tis only fear what keeps em quiet. Pretence and sham the lot of it. Thou art noh the keeper of truth, but the father of lies!'

Flickin the tongue, I weaved and slithered the body about while the Prelate looked upon me, wide-orbed and perspirin, as I done my fierce menacin snake dance upon him.

'I know the truth,' hissed I, 'and know the only way it could happen is that ye have forced yersen upon her.'

Mask in hand I slipped behind him, standin betwix the window and the chair. He kep swivelin his neck this-way-a-that for it made him fierce jittery noh bein able to keep an eye upon me. Restin my hands on the back of his chair, I leant into his lug.

'I knowt the truth for allway! I conjured it as a child. Night after night lyin in bed, I closed the orbs and it would come to me. I knowt it allway, since afore I can mind.'

I begun runnin my fingers through his hair, soft and tender-like.

'Whispered ye like this into her ear, did ye noh? Whispered and blathered into her lug just as I am whisperin into yers.'

I got right up close to him then, flickin the tongue round the rim of his ear. He whipped the skull away when I done that and tried to leap and hop some with the chair aneath him

164

and all. Shufflin alongside him, I placed the hand upon him so as he could move no further.

'Where's thou rushin off to then?'

Bringin the mask over his shoulder, I creeped the beak across his skull so as it hooked round his cheek.

'I'm the great and frightsome Prelate,' sayt I, caressin his mug with the beak. 'Howbe?'

Leavin the mask there, I brought my gob back round the further side of his skull.

'Her black hair were aneath yer neb, no? The smell of her were intoxicatin and sent yer skull into a dwam – into a rage of lust and longin.'

I took a whiff of his sparse and scraggly hair.

'What didst thou say to her?' enquizzened I. 'Calt her a whore as ye done now and took her hair into yer fist?'

I wound the thin greyin wisps of his hair betwix my fingers and pulled his skull back.

'*I will put the word of God inside thee, the spirit of the Lord shall cleanse thy womb.*'

I begun movin his skull back-a-fort, as though it were joltin with the force of my body behind him.

'Recited from the Book as ye forced yersen upon her, no? *Lord make thee a curse and an oath among thy people, the water that causeth the curse shall enter into thee, and become bitter and thy belly shall swell and thee, woman, shall be a curse among thy people.*'

I wrenched his head faster and more violent.

'As ye reached yer unravellin – the expulsion of yer lust and longin – ye begun drawin the beak across her skin, slicin into her cheek and peckin into her flesh. That's how she come to have those marks upon her, is it noh, snake?'

165

I begun draggin the mask across his cheek, light and slow at first then harder and deeper till the Prelate started wrigglin and squirmin in the chair.

'Hallion!' raged he, spittin upon the floor. 'Scourge of Hell!'

I pulled at his cloak till it become loose, whereupon I begun peckin him upon the back, betwix the shoulder blades.

'Has done this upon her?' enquizzened I, joltin his skull back-a-fort and peckin him till the beak become damp and bloody as he howled and cursed upon me. 'Whore!' sayt I, bringin the beak over his shoulder and smearin the blood across his cheek. 'Then ye were done,' sayt I, thrustin his skull away. 'She collapsed aneath ye and ye left her there bleedin and limp. Ye'd taken her tongue for she'd noh spake from that day fort. Ye'd stolen the tongue of the child and her voice crawled inside her, it hid and quivered deep in the depths of her womb. But I am that voice from the womb and it no longer quivers but quakes!'

I come back round forta face him, throwin the mask upon the table.

'That is what I saw in the night as a child, imaginin what ye done upon her, and each spell it ended the same – her turnin the skull over her shoulder as though it were I what were behind her. Lookin straight into mine eyes, she'd mouth muted words. I strained to hear what she sayt but naught come from her gob. I ner heard the words she were tryin to tell me, for ye had stolen her tongue – snake!'

He raised the skull to me, mumblin blather-spake I could-noh understand.

'What?' sayt I. 'Spake up, thou art swallowin thy words.'

'*Kill the child*,' sayt he. 'That is what she sayt, night your misbegotten sen arrived to stain and blacken the Quag. *Have mercy*, sayt she, *kill the child*.'

I come back agin the table, disturbin the butterfly what rose up to flutter some upon the air.

'Thine own mother wanted ye dead.'

'That's noh true.'

'Is it not?' scoffed he. 'Thou knows it is the truth, thou knows.'

'It matters none anywise,' sayt I, the tongue becomin thick and the face feelin as though it bin set alight. 'Who is that woman to me? A ghost! It is ye what doesnoh know the truth.'

'Thou shalt enlighten me.'

'Aye, snake, I will. For I werenoh born of her, backwise or otherwise. I were born of no soul and come from no body – I gave birth to mysen!'

The Prelate looked at me slantwise.

'I come noh from man nor woman. The cord what come from my belly flailed about in the emptiness, I were nourished on the night and suckled by the void, I were birthed from blackness and the stars!'

'Halfwit and aberration,' sayt he. 'Just like her, thou art mad.'

Sweat come drippin from his chin, the damp hair clingin to his pale mug. It were fleetin, but I caught the Prelate's brumal blue eyes flicker sneaky-like twort the pot upon the stove. Cockin the eye, I become all curious and the like.

'What have we here?' enquizzened I.

His dark and sorry lookin sen averted mine eyes, sheepish some and wily. Truth be tolt, I'd forgotted all about the pot, it'd become somethin constant and soothin what droned and babbled away in the corner of the room.

The bubblin become louder as I approached the stove, the pot near coverin its entire plinth. The butterfly come flutterin about the shoulder, followin me forta have a squint as well. The lid were dancin and jigglin from the pressure aneath and, as I raised it, a gush of steam wafted across the mug. It took a spell to realise what I were lookin upon, pale and bony as it were with the flesh comin away in parts. Jouncin up-a-down in the pot, the gaunt and ghostlike skull of Levi's calf were bein jostled about upon the bubbles what rose from its blackened bottom – a leaden, opaque eye starin up-a-me from aneath the undulatin surface. Without thinkin, I plunged the hand into the scoldin water which were a scatter-brained thing ado, sure and certain. No sooner were my hand in than it were out again and I were howlin with the pain and leppin about the room. Placin it aneath the pit of mine arm, I squeezed it tight and felt the pain spreadin through the limbs like it were takin possession of my body. When it reached the skull, I thought I may keel over for I'd become fierce faint and qualmish. All this were of great amusement to himsen a course, and he laughed in pathetic bloody puffs and snorts.

'Thou art a feeble-minded child,' sayt he. 'Should have been left in the Wastes, abandoned to wither upon the rocks.'

I were in too much pain to say aught, busy leppin and hollerin bout the room with the hand feelin as though it were meltin from mine arm and all. It were becomin red and blistered and throbbed like my heart were inside it – *Duhm-duhm, duhm-dhum, dhum-dhum*, sayt the wee heart inside my hand. It were true what the Prelate sayt, I were feeble-minded and dozy, I've knowt that a longspell, but a soul must make the most of what he has – what else be there for it? I wouldnoh bother addin that to *The Philosophy of the Wastelands* for it is an empty axiom and is noh worthy.

Anywise, instead of respondin to the Prelate what I did were I closed mine eyes and tolt mysen the pain were naught, for I were a fierce wild beast-child what could control himsen, and so I concentrated on pushin the pain back inside while takin great deep breaths – for ye'll find that helps some. Grabbin a raggedy piece of clout near the stove, I swaddled the hand and turnt back to the Prelate who'd begun recitin passages from the Book.

'I cannoh abide those words any longer,' sayt I, through clenched teeth, 'best shut thy gob.'

But he wouldnoh listen, so I raised the unscorched hand and pointed to the corner of the room. He followed mine arm, becomin quiet a spell afore turnin back to face me, the prayers comin louder still.

'Right, thou leaves me no choice,' sayt I.

When the Prelate had wanted to quieten or punish me as a child all he had ado were point to the corner of the room. It were a dreadful and frightenin thing to see his arm raised and the finger pointin there – even now, lookin upon it made my stomach turn and tighten. Marchin over I crouched down and lifted the loose board aneath which the box were kep. Turnin twort him, I raised it into the air, shakin and rattlin it about so as he knowt sure and certain what were comin. He refused to look upon it but continued babblin words from the Book.

'Tolt ye,' sayt I, comin back to him, 'cannoh say I didnoh warn ye.'

Placin the box upon the floor I took out the pliers and the mouthpiece and helt em afore him.

'Mind ye this?'

Naught.

'Course ye does, many the day it were used upon me. Tis yer turn now.'

169

I helt the mouthpiece afore him, what were used to keep the gob open so as a soul could get at the tongue with the pliers. Anywise, I wiggled it about afore his lips as though I were tryin to feed a wee reluctant bairn. I made buzzin sounds like a bee what were tryin to fly into his gob in a round-about and loopsome way.

'Zzzzzzzzzzzzzzzzzz, zzzzzzzzzzzzz,' sayt I, spiralin the mouthpiece twort him.

The Prelate seemed uninterested in openin the gob.

'Come now, this will be one way another, well thou knows,' sayt I, jigglin it about some more.

He kep the lips pursed good and tight, what were the very same I done when I were a child. So I poked and prodded his flesh with the sword forta persuade him. When the gob come open to holler, I rammed the mouthpiece into it so as it could-noh close again.

'Now the tongue,' sayt I.

But the tongue werenoh fortcomin neither. Insertin the pliers into his gob, his pink and fleshy slug begun dartin this-way-a-that tryin to escape the metal jaws – *Click, click, click* sayt the pliers as I brought em agether without the tongue inbetwix. It werenoh long though till I had it clamped for there is noh much room in a gob for a tongue to hide or escape. Anywise, I stretched it outside his open maw then swapped hands so as I could pick up the vice. Given that the right hand were fierce sore on account of the fact it bin cooked and boiled in the pot, the tightenin of the vice were slow and laborious work as I had to use the other hand forta screw it upon the tongue, what felt fierce strange and unnatural as ye yesen will know if ye ever tried usin the wrong hand ado somethin. After a spell, I managed to clamp it on the tongue good and proper, and

170

let go of the vice all agether. The weight of it helt the tongue stretched from the mouth and caused great distress to the soul what wore it. The saliva would drip as though ye were a rabid dog and yer tongue felt like it were bein torn inchmeal from yer skull. The soul what wore the vice made strange gurglin sounds tryin to breathe and rid himsen of the saliva what gathered in all corners and crevices. All agether it were a fierce painful and tormentin ordeal what sent the skull barmy.

'Stay there,' I tolt him.

Turnin round I picked up the sword from the table – seein me do this the Prelate attempted to spake, though praps he were just recitin from the Book, it were hard to tell.

'I cannoh understand a thing thou says,' sayt I. 'If thou doesnoh learn to pronounce thy words how can ye expect God to hear thy prayers?'

He tried to escape me, slidin the chair backwise across the floor. When he could go no further he kep workin the feet, slidin em back-a-fort as though he thought he may be able to push himsen right through the wall. His eyes were raised to the top of the skull for that were the only way he could see me, as straightenin the neck with the vice attached were a painful and, after a spell, impossible thing ado. It were an arrestin sight, him sat there agin the wall, head bowed by the vice with the wings pressed agin the window what rose above his skull like a queer and quiversome moon. I musta bin a sight for his dark and sorry sen as well, comin twort him in the whale flesh with the shades of the butterflies bloomin upon me. Takin hold of the vice, I placed the sword aneath his tongue and looked into his wet and spiritless orbs.

'So as ye can preach no more,' sayt I.

Pullin the vice down as far as I could, I ran the length of the sword agin his slaverin pink lump till it come clear out his gob and there rose from inside his most holy and tongueless sen a godawful muffled hollerin. It were a watery sound what come from his mouth with the gurglin of the blood and so fort – it sounded as though there were a spirit inside him what were both drownin and burnin at the same spell.

I helt the vice out in front of him so as he could stare upon his very own tongue – a peculiar circumstance what happens to but a few rare souls. Thing were though, he kep his eyes closed, for he were concentratin on the pain and the blood what flooded his gullet. I kep vigilant, followin the movements of his skull so as when he did open the lids it were the first thing he saw – surprisement itsen he were, the orbs becomin wide and unbelievin. *What's thou doin there?* he were thinkin as he looked upon the bloody mound of flesh what lay betwix the pincers. *Tis a most unnatural and troublesome sight to gawp upon one's own tongue, sure and certain.*

I helt the vice up to mine own gob and shook it about some, as though I were spakin with the tongue of the Prelate.

'Yibbity bla, bla, sin and repentance,' sayt I. 'Yabbity bla, bla, Hell and damnation. Yibbity bla, bla, bla, blather-spake and gibberish!'

He didnoh find the impersonation amusin a course, for he were busy reelin and yawin – bemoanin his very unfortunate lot, I expect. I turnt the tongue twort me so as I could look upon it good and proper.

'Imagine this wee lump of flesh what scarce spaked for itsen could hold all Grathico unto slavery.'

'Aaarhhh gaahh gaaahhhhlll,' sayt he.

'Hush!' sayt I, for I were ponderin hard upon the tongue's mysterious powers.

'Aaarhhh gaahhlllgahh gaaahhhhllll!'

'Quiet thou! I cannoh concentrate with all yer carry-on and clamour!'

'Gargle argle, blather-patter!' bewailed he.

'Right!' sayt I, raisin the vice and marchin twort him, fixin to clobber him over the skull with his very own tongue.

Afore I could reach him though the butterfly overtook me, flutterin past the shoulder it scuttered rickety squiggles through the air as it headed twort his bloody and moanful sen. Seein it comin twort him, the Prelate started with the foot again, slidin it back-a-fort in a vainsome attempt to flee. When it were close, the butterfly stopped flutterin and – without ditherin – flew straight into the Prelate's gob.

Rushin over, I peered inside his gory spake-hole and saw the creature flappin round the back of his gullet – its vibrant, luminous wings churnin the blood and gack what gathered there. Leanin fort as far as his tied hands would allow, the Prelate coughed and splattered blood, tryin to rid his throat of the butterfly. When it wouldnoh budge, he tilted the skull back, for that seemed the best way for him to draw breath. I become enthralled watchin the creature twistin and turnin inside. It's wings had become soaked in blood and were drained of colour. Truth be, it looked like there were a spirit – a conflation of tormented spirits – writhin in the craggy depths of the Prelate's dark and squishy numbles. The washed-out patterns of the wings looked like dull eyes starin up-a-me afore they rolled and folded back into his gullet, like his throat were a spirit mill what churned and grinded anguished souls back into his gizzards. The sound from his gullet were unnervin, sure and certain, a harrowed cackle mixed with the beatin of the wings inside – *flitter-burble-slosh, flitter-burble-slosh*, sayt he, cep very fast and gurgly.

The butterfly disappeared down the Prelate's gullet all agether, cuttin off his air and causin his body to become rigid with the mug pointin skyward and the eyes wide like he'd just spied God Himsen curled up inbetwix the rafter beams of the ceilin. His feet slid slow and laggard across the floor as though they'd become fierce heavy in a sudden, for it werenoh God a course, but Death what were descendin upon him – Mortality hersen had come, cold and beguilin, forta cast him unto shade. There were horror in his orbs at the sight of her lush dark wings unfurlin above him – tender and invitin they reached out forta hap him up snug-like and cosy in a smothersome embrace what would coddle him through all eternity. Slowise, the feet growt still upon the floor, the Prelate's body slumped agin the chair and his blue cormorant eyes become fixed – locked upon abstraction, starin through and beyond me.

I stood there a spell, lookin upon the Prelate's lifeless mug till the butterfly come up – peepin its skull above his opened maw it fluttered some forta free itsen of the blood gathered upon its wings. Walkin in circles across his chin and cheek, his neb and forehead, it wove wee bloody and concentric footprints across the length of his mortal skull – a secret script sown across his ashen face, consignin his body to the next world.

Things become quiet and uncommon. A twilight of sorts settled inside my skull, sun flickered into mine eyes from betwix the bodies of the butterflies and I become aware of the low murmur and tumult from the Grathicans out-side. Possessed by a spirit of the Wastes, I raised the sword and – marchin upon the lifeless body slumped across the

174

chair – I took to severin the Prelate's head from his shoulders. It were done in a haze of gore and fury and, afore I knowt it, I stood sprent and welterin in his blood, his skull hangin from a clump of thin grey hair clutched betwix the fingers of my tremblin hand. Impalin his skull upon the hook, I turnt for the door, the butterfly risin forta follow me. On my way out, I heaved the pot from the heat and listened to it clang and clatter to the ground. Steam risin from the water, I left the skull of the calf upon the floor so as to keep an eye upon Grathico and lay a curse upon his house.

Comin out the door, the butterflies scattered hither-thither and I found the Grathicans where I left em. I'd the feelin they'd become fierce quiet and still upon mine exit. *Howbe?* sayt I, inside my skull. Outside my skull, it were all silence and tension a course, with no soul sayin aught cep the sly hushper of the wind scutterin through the narrows of Grathico. The wind blew across me, creepin up the stairs onto the porch, brushin my hair to the side like a kindsome old mother. I thought praps it were tellin me to go – *Best leave*, it were sayin, givin the old hair a lick afore sendin me on my way – *off ye go there beast-boy, take care yersen and all. Mind thee well, for it is a fierce cruel and lonesome world out there, sure and certain – keep thy wits about thee.* I started down the stairs. *Hoy!* whispered the wind, stoppin me in my tracks – *Give my best to the spirits of the Wastes, willint ye?*

'Aye,' sayt I, half-loud, 'I will a course.'

I come down the stairs and walked down the wee path, wings flutterin all about, for the creatures werenoh just upon the house but were spilt across the porch and down the steps as well, smotherin all the ground what surrounded. Comin through the gate I stood a spell – a bloodied butterfly skittin

175

about the shoulders and the skull of the Prelate hangin upsy-down from the hook in my hand. His grey and scraggly hair hung in clumps – unwantin to leave the sanctity of his home it were lookin to take root in the consecrated ground of Grath-ico. The souls of the village stood starin upon me, gawkin upon the horror what exited the house. Their eyes become fixed upon the skull a course and there rose a muffled gasp from among the gawpin crowd – hands comin across gobs with the pure astonishment of it all. From the corner of mine eye I saw a cluster of butterflies fall from the awnin of the house and scatter in all directions. Takin that as my cue, I turnt from the Closemen and the Stone Thrower and all the souls of Grathico and begun walkin my creaky and improba-ble bones slowise down the street.

Kitter-katter-kitter-katter-kitter-katter, sayt the butterflies, liftin from the house and plumin in a flittery cloud above. Without lookin I knowt the Grathicans had come too, movin out slowise into the street. Passin through the old and familiar ground I saw a few souls scatterin and dartin for cover, scared of a wee beast-boy and a few butterflies they were – mooncalves.

Down the way a wean and his goose had run to the edge of the street, the boy's chin were skyward, lookin upon the butterflies. Geese were important in the life of a wean for each boy had to take care of his own, they had to feed and groom em and could ner leave their dwellins without em in tow. Durin the warmer days they would sleep next their bird in the wee house wherein it were kep. When the child were growt and it were time to become a man he would have to kill and consume his bird, turnin his back on the weantime he would change his garms and become initiated into the rites of the sodality – he would become a Grathican, true and proper.

'Howbe?' sayt I, comin alongside the child.

Takin a few steps back he regarded me a spell afore dippin the wee pale mug. The goose honked some, swingin the beak side-a-side.

'That yer goose then?'

Wee nods of the skull.

'Does it have a name?'

Starin up-a-me he blinked the orbs some.

'Well?'

He shrugged the shoulders.

'Me neither,' sayt I.

I saw a shadow scutter behind a house, the child's mother no doubt, so I turnt to walk away.

'Bird!' shouted the boy.

'What?' enquizzened I, turnin round.

'Bird, is what I call him, or Flap-a-Wings.'

'That so?'

The boy nodded very adamant-like.

'I teached him.'

'What's that?'

'Flap-a-Wings, I teached him.'

'Teached him what?'

'Everythin.'

'He's a fine goose, sure and certain, thou hast done well.'

The boy nodded the skull afore turnin to look upon his bird. Old Flap-a-Wings had the beak turnt the other way and gave a wee honk as though he knowt what were bein sayt upon him but were none too bothered all the same, as though praise were heaped upon him every next day and he'd become bored by it.

When I turnt back to the boy he started noddin again.

'If ye keep rattlin yer skull like that it may well fall off,' sayt I, swingin the Prelate back-a-fort upon the hook.

He stayed still and quiet lookin upon the skull hangin upsy-down.

'Thou fetors some.'

'That so?'

'Aye.'

'Expect I do, good or bad?'

He shrugged the shoulders afore castin the wee sly orbs slantwise up the street to look upon the Grathicans what clustered there.

'Art thou a spirit of the Wastes?' enquizzened he in a soft and quavery voice.

I thought upon his question some.

'Aye,' sayt I, 'guess I am. Art thou noh afeared?'

He shook his skull.

'Thou art a big man?'

He shrugged the shoulders.

'I cannoh hear ye,' sayt I.

The goose gave a short sharp honk.

'Seems Flap-a-Wings is a big man, art thou?'

He nodded some, very sheepish mind.

'Noh with the skull with the tongue,' sayt I. 'Art thou a big man?'

'Aye!' sayt he loud and clear, with the wee chest swollen and the shoulders back and all.

'Good lad.'

I went to put my hand atop the boy's skull but I heard the mother gasp in the shadows. As I turnt to walk off, I saw her scutter from her hidin place and drag the boy back to safety – old Flap-a-Wings seemed none too pleased though, honkin and hallooin and so fort.

178

I begun to hear murmurs from the souls behind – very upset and sorrowful I imagine they was at the thoughts of me leavin and all. When I come to the limits I paused and looked long and hard upon the stones what separated the village from the Wilds – after considerin it a spell, I raised the skull and, with fierce joy and relief, I stepped across the borderlands and marched out of Grathico.

I'd noh gone far when I felt a sharp pain in the shoulder and heard a dull thud upon the ground behind me. Turnin round, I saw a mass of bodies spread out lengthwise along the limits of the village, starin hard upon me. They'd come out of the shadowy nooks and crenels of Grathico to bid me farewell. Withy and Throstle were among em, standin agether near one end, glum and wordless. The Stone Thrower lifted his wee arm and hurled another rock, but this spell he were wide of his mark and I watched it skitter along the ground, impotent and unprofitable.

'Get thee back!' bawled he with all his wee potent sen. 'Get thee back, Beastht! The Unholy shall noh walk here! Back! Git!' hissed he, hurlin another stone.

I'd turnt and moved off afore it hit the ground – with the Prelate's skull in my hand and a plague of butterflies above, I walked back into the Wastelands.

XIX

I'd noh tolt ye about the blackness and the stars and all that, for I thought ye may think me a deranged thing from the swamp. Truth is, I couldnoh reconcile mysen to the blood what ran through my veins and so I'd conjured mine own origins. I'd willed mysen from a celestial womb of mine own creation so that none could lay claim to me. A soul must come from somewhere and I'd noh seen aught what I belonged to, cep the dark sky and stars above – and Levi a course, now she'd come ashore. So that were for allway the story I'd tolt mysen and it may well be the truth for all ye know – it were the truth behind the truth, so a spake.

I were traipsin back through the Wastes a course, headin twort Melas and hersen the Leviathan with the Prelate's pale and sickly mug swingin upsy-down upon the hook. He musta bin fierce dizzy with the orbs wide open, swayin back-a-fort and lookin upon the world wrong ways up and all –

180

Wooohhh there, beast-boy, sayt he, *the gizzards – what bin left way back there in Grathico – have started to feel a wee bit queasy.* Anywise, when we come to the cliff I spied Levi in a distance laid out upon the sand where I'd left her, cep gulls had arrived in our absence forta feast upon her flesh and take advantage of her in her state of abandonment. They was swarmin in a cloud above, like they do Melas when there's a great flock of fishes swimmin neath the surface. Circlin some, they swooped upon Levi forta plunge their beaks into her flesh while others stayed perched upon her flank, peckin at her blubber, squawkin and carryin-on like all their prayers bin answered.

Scramblin down the cliff to the shore I were confronted by a great farrago of gulls and butterflies, for the birds were very reluctant to leave, as ye may well expect. They was tryin to stand their ground, squawkin and flappin the wings very menacin and frightsome and the like – *Kkkkkraaaahhhk, kkkkraaaaahhhk,* sayt they, fierce nettled at havin their feast interrupted. Some took to the sky, tryin to take the flesh out each other's gobs as they went, others begun peckin like mad, gluttin the gullet with as much whale blubber as possible afore they was evicted – greedy mooncalves.

'Yaaaah!' bawled I, whizzin the skull of the Prelate through the air forta shoo and scatter em.

Slow and reluctant, they begun to disperse, though some kep circlin above, squawkin and makin an unholy show of emsens while others hopped about upon the sand pretendin they just happened to be there, as though it were pure chance and serendipity what had brought em to our shores. Pokin round, all nonchalant and the like, they made as though there were a number of things what were of great interest to em, while at the same spell keepin a close eye upon me and the colossal mound of flesh what had sent em barmy.

'Yaaaaah!' shrieked I, chargin em. 'I'm noh that dozy!'

Put out and all, they hopped away from me upon very scrawny pegs with the feathery rumps swingin this-way-a-that.

'Krrraaaak, kkraaaak,' squawked they, as though I'd come for their weans.

The gulls moved off, cep this one article what were takin his own time to scamper and payin no heed to mysen nor the butterflies. I waited till he raised his wee glutinous beak from her flesh afore brandishin the Prelate's skull with all I may, while hollerin and hallooin and so fort. The gull swung his beak back-a-fort, wantin to catch a glimpse of me with both eyes, as though he didnoh believe a bold and scraggly mudlark such as mysen could exist. Puffin out the chest, very cheeky-like, he begun squawkin till his wee gullet become hoarse – *Kkkkrrraaaak!* sayt he, afore plungin the beak back into the whale. Comin up again he helt a large string of blubber in his gob – *See this*, sayt he, flickin the beak and jogglin the blubber side-a-side, *I've taken one last lump of flesh – what ye gonna do bout that then?* Turnin from me, as though I were the Devil himsen, he took to the air upon very laboured and lackadaisy wings, weighed down as he were by a belly full of whale. Brazen these birds, swear to God.

Once they was all gone and the butterflies settled, I turnt to Levi.

'See what I've brought ye?' sayt I, holdin up the hook.

Blackness and the stars, beast-boy?

'What?' enquizzened I, wee bit sheepish.

Notions!

'I got carried away is all – look!'

182

Movin round her, I raised the skull further so as she may see what I brought her.

That is very thoughtful, thou art a gentleman, sure and certain but I'd rather noh look upon it, if it's all the same to ye.

Starin upon the skull, I shrugged the shoulders.

'Wait here,' I tolt her. 'I'll come back to thee soon.'

Off I scuttled, skull in hand with the lone and loyal butterfly followin close behind. I were headed for the Sheers, that part of the Wastes what drops away from the Quag without end in a lonesome, dwam-makin wall of rock and looks as though it bin chiselled by the hand of Lucifer himsen. The Sheers were naught cep rock and more rock, till ye reached Melas a course, who waited all impatient and turgid at the bottom, batterin her restless watery sen agin the edge of the world. It were sayt the Sheers were so tall ye could throw a rock from the top and run to the bottom in time to catch it. Noh sure how that works mysen, cause; first-all, there were no place ye could run and, second-all, if it took that long for a stone to fall to the bottom ye'd be a grey and oldenin beast-boy what could scarce walk let alone run by the time ye got there. Anywise, that were what were sayt – dozy if ye enquizzen me.

Standin at the edge of the Sheers I looked upon Melas, followin her way out in a distance where her dark vacillatin sen become very thin and faint till she disappeared into the sky all agether. It were quite the view up there and I thought the Prelate may like to look upon it himsen – rightways up a course. He were fierce hefty and I were forced to use both hands to raise him afore me – one upon the hook and the other cradled at the back of his skull like he were a wee bairn and all.

Turnin round some I showed him the view.

'There ye go now,' sayt I, 'Melas hersen, and the vain and wicked world what stretches beyond.'

Thing were though, he seemed uninterested in what I showed him and wouldnoh look upon it but kep the eyes fixed to the sky. The mouth were open and gormless, while the opaque orbs were glassy with thin red veins runnin over the whites, snakin their way twort the blue. There were a watery gleam upon em what looked as though a tear were trapped or clusterin there.

'Pull thy blubberin sen agether!' I scolded him. 'Tis late for that now and very unbecomin for a skull of thy stature!'

I turnt him back to the sea.

'How bout a wee swim then?' enquizzened I. 'A wee dip forta blow the cobwebs away. What's thou say?'

The skull nodded some, bobbin up-a-down upon the hook.

'That's the spirit,' sayt I. 'The hook will take ye to the very depths of the sea from where ye can stare up at the world from thy watery tomb. Ye may even spy mysen and Levi swimmin back-a-fort above ye from time to time. What's more, thou willst have the great privilege of watchin the fishes nibble upon yer very own orbs and all. What's thou think of that then?'

This spell, the pasty scraggle-haired skull were all vigorous and the like with the noddin, as though the thoughts of havin fishes nibblin upon his orbs were near the best thing he ever heard.

'Right so,' sayt I, 'to the fishes it is.'

Comin back, I begun swingin the arm and twistin the hips to-a-fro so as to build momentum. The butterfly fluttered out the way to give me room and observe me in a distance. Whippin the body round, I made two full rotations circlewise till I come close to the edge of the Sheers and let go of the skull.

'Yyyyyaaaaaaaaaahhh!' sayt I as it come from my hands and spun through the air – hook then skull, hook then skull, and so fort.

Watchin his mug and wild grey hair twirlin through the air, I imagined I could hear him hollerin and bawlin as he plunged into the sea. The scream become loud then soft, dependin whether it were his gob or the hook what were to the fore;

AAAAHHHHHaaaaahhhhhAAAAAAHHHHHaaaaahhhhh, sayt he.

I ran fort so as I could see the skull be swallowed up by Melas' gapin black maw – for no matter how hard I throwt it, the Sheers were so high I'd noh be able to see it break the surface lest I lay upon the belly and peered over the edge. I followed the arc of the skull till it become but a wee speck, tumblin twort the water.

'Sploshshshshsh!' sayt I, as it plunged into the sea.

I stayed on the belly, watchin the sea gurglin and bubblin aneath, imaginin it were a vast pot of boilin water decoctin the evil from within the Prelate's skull, just as he himsen had done to the calf. I become enthralled starin into Melas' great squally blackness, watchin her white spittle spider-webbin across the dark swells of her body – dissipatin and reformin but ner in the same pattern, ner repeatin hersen. *Kahhhbush, bush, bush, bush, kahhhhbammm,* sayt she, hurlin hersen upon the Sheers with the unendin delight she took in rammin her skull agin very hard and immovable things. From the heighth I were, though, it become muffled and sounded like she were singin an old cradle song to me. I thought I could feel her great violent wallops agin the Quag as gentle bumps that reached me through the rocks way up top of the Sheers. She were lullin me into a dwam with the violent undulations of her body and the patterns what formed and waned atop her. I begun to feel as though the whole Quag were undulatin with her, till the butterfly come flitterin bout the skull and makin a fuss – *Raise thysen*, sayt the creature, *thou dost noh have time for this haver and tripe, for there are still things to be done afore ye can return to the Leviathan.* It were right a course, so I shook the skull and raised mysen.

XX

The bothy seemed frightened and quivery as I approached, sequestered there on its lonesome, squeezed betwix the large black rocks what loomed either side. The gizzards were all atwist as I drew near, for I'd noh bin back since afore the crone come to tell about the woman and the whale. It seemed a different place all agether, like it had changed its skin somewise, like it bin torn down and rebuilt by hateful spirits. It seemed a whole other beast-boy had lived there – once upon a spell, long, long ago – and even he were gone, and it were just his ghost what wandered round and round its four crumblin walls.

'Boo!' sayt I, as I come across the threshold.

Inside were a musty, charnel foetor – I'd no clue what I were goin ado but, after standin there a spell lookin about mysen like a mooncalf, I begun clusterin all the bric-a-brac and odds and bobs twort the centre of the bothy. Takin the

187

soft and straw things I'd used as beddin, I spread em round the base forta serve as kindlin. Bringin a large rock from outside, I raised it above the skull and brought it down upon the cupboard, shatterin and splinterin the brittle oldenin timber. I took to twistin it apart with the hands and placin large skelfs of wood round the tinder forta form a pyramid, the likes of which flames like to climb and grow. I were become feverish, smashin and breakin and draggin things hither-thither, for I were makin a pyre from the debris of my hitherto peculiar existence.

Takin the drawers from the old chester, I come across the box where I kep the butterfly I'd taken from the sacristy, around which I'd wound the long black hair I'd found when first I come to the bothy. It stopped me, sure and certain. I'd forgotted all about it, truth be tolt, in my frenzy and haste I'd forgotted it were there. Takin the lid off, the butterfly were just as I left it, but it were the hair encirclin the singed wings what had mine attention – it lay curled up, very particular and attentive upon the cloth I'd laid at the bottom. Takin it betwix the thumb and forefinger I drew it out inchmeal from the box – it kep comin and comin, unfurlin without end and so fort. It'd bin a longspell since I last looked upon it for I didnoh like to disturb it much. Holdin it afore me, with the arm stretched above the skull, it near come to the floor from the sheer length of it and all. Placin the box and the butterfly atop the pyre, I took the strand of hair to the threshold and stepped outside the bothy. Pinched betwix the fingers I helt it there a spell, watchin it thresh and flail in the wind as though it were fierce anxious to make tracks. I felt it tuggin upon the skin till it slipped through the fingers and were gone – whisked away by unseen hands and swept across the Wastelands. I'd like to think the wind took it across the barren rocks, past the sands all the way to the sea where it come to rest upon Melas' undulatin spine. That'd be a soothin thought a course, but more like than noh, it got no further-an the Wastes – like as noh, it got caught in the brambles on the way and become wrapped round some wispy thing-a-ma-gig I'd noh yet had the chance to eat. Chances are it's still there, swaddled round some thorny stem, flayin about in the wind and makin wee wavin motions at the sea.

Comin back inside, I took up clusterin the odds and ends to the centre of the bothy. When I were finished, I lit the kindlin at the base of the pyre. The flames took slow at first, wee nervous tendrils strugglin to come to life, soon though they were all woooosh and crackle as they growt stronger, bitin down on the wood and twistin round the tinder in an ancient, dwam-makin dance. I stayed there as long as I could though soon had to leave on account of the fact the smoke had begun to choke me. Comin outside I stood in a distance, watchin flames rise in the window and smoke pour from every nook and cranny as though the bothy were bleedin grey and wispy blood what flowed upward twort the sky. *Kkkkkssshhhhhhhhh!* sayt the window, causin me to flinch some as it shattered from the pressure of the ghosts inside what were tryin to escape afore their ethereal, invisible rumps become scorched and inflamed.

I stayed there till the bothy were engulfed, till the ghosts what writhed and twisted inside the black smoke were torn apart by the wind and driven backwise twort the sea. The thoughts of the bothy burnin to the ground ignited a fire in my belly and a wee seditious delight in my chest. I stayed till the roof collapsed, till I knowt sure and certain it were gone, then

189

I turnt my back upon it for allway and for aye and marched mysen through the Wastes twort the shore, forta lie with the Leviathan.

Thistledown were in flight as I walked through the Wilds, for it were the time of year it come loose from the stem and begun driftin cross the Quag, like tufts of snow blown sidewards upon the wind. I stood at Quag's end, breathin in the faint scent of smoke and watchin thistledown sail over the edge of the cliff, heedless of gravity, hopin to fertilise the barren sands and the saline brine of the sea. The Thistle Drift, as it were knowt in Grathico, signalled a change in seasons, a shift from bitterest winter to warmer climes. It were sayt that the plant absorbed some of the spirits of the Wastes afore expungin em come the springtide and it were this unburdenin what brought the softer weather.

Anywise, I were back to where it were – more or less – that I first saw Levi. The butterflies lay upon her a course, a few flutterin hither-thither, blithesome and lackadaisy. On her further side the poles tilted out the sand, all broken and sorry-lookin. I could see the tracks I'd walked and that come away from her this-way-a-that – a map of sorts it were, a chronicle of my time spent with hersen the Leviathan. Most of it couldnoh be seen a course from all the commotion and unwanted feet what had tread upon the shore, but there were parts what remained. Comin out the patches of dark and roiled shore ye could see my footsteps betwix Levi and the scorched sand where I'd lit the fire. Ye could see the pile of blankets I'd used to keep the sea upon her lyin near the hollow wherein the yawl were kep. Ye could see the grave I'd dug for the Grathicans and the great red V of the Leviathan's last breath stretched upon our sorry and lonesome ait. A story of sorts it were, one what plotted

190

the arrival, slaughter and posthumous exploits of mysen and the Great Fish.

Comin down the rocks, first thing I done were run my hand upon her flank, causin the butterflies to scatter some so as to make room for mine affection. Aneath my hand I noticed she were changin – it were near imperceptible but the blubber had begun to slacken betwix the great armature of her bones.

'Just ye and me now,' sayt I, strokin her aneath the gob.

Melas broke loud upon the shore when I sayt that, fierce hurt and indignant so she were – *Mind me and all, dost thou?* I took no notice a course, for a great lethargy had come over me. My bones had become heavy and my blood claggy, for I'd growt weary of the violence what ran constant-like through my veins – that were the illness from which I suffered, so it seemed to me, that were mine own prognosis, if ye wants to know the truth.

XXI

The sounds of the world were made remote by the ruin of Levi's flesh. Happed up inside her, I listened to the rumblin of the sea and tried to pick the different squawks of the fowl what mulled about the skies, till I become aware of sundry voices tinklin in a distance. Stirrin some, I peered out the great wound of her belly and saw the dark and jagged shadow of the raggedy souls of Grathico standin upon the mull. On the sand already, Withy were lollopin as fast as his gangly pegs would carry him; hands over head, he waved and hallooed forta warn me the Grathicans were come and my very wayward and irredeemable sen were in grave danger. Throstle were trotttin along behind him, blather-spake and jarble issuin from his excitable gob. A parcel of gowks were upon their heels chasin close behind, and it werenoh long afore Throstle were rounded up and they turnt their attention to his great and spindly sen whose clumsy strides couldnoh escape em.

Leppin upon him like dogs, Withy's long frame come to ground – a felled tree brought upon the shore.

As soon as they was captured the rest of the Grathicans spilt from the mull and come upon the sand. I'd thought praps I'd ner rise again but stay there inside the Leviathan for allway and for aye, snug and happed in her flesh but the blood become roiled soon as I lay sight on em. Couldnoh leave things be, could they? The Prelate for the Leviathan seemed fair to me.

Slippin from her guts, I heard the high-pitched and squealy voice of a child risin over the drone of the men – he couldnoh be seen as yet but it were the First Stone Thrower, sure and certain. Clusterin my things about me – the sword and spears and such – I begun pacin up-a-down the sand. I didnoh look upon the Grathicans as I marched but instead concentrated all the rancour what churned in my gizzards upon the ground afore me.

'Canst thou see em?' enquizzened I of Melas.

Aye, sayt she.

'Where are they?'

Up a ways a bit.

I could hear the voices comin nearer as I wore a track betwix Levi and the sea.

Wait, sayt Melas.

From the corner of mine eye I spied a pall of bodies movin across the sand.

Noh yet, sayt she.

The nerves were buildin inside me, they were pent up and jittery like a wee prickly animal yennin to escape and wreak havoc upon the shore.

Nooooowww! roared the sea.

193

Melas broke upon the sand with a whoosh and I turnt on my heel and charged the Grathicans.

'Yaaaaaaaaahhhhhhhhh!' bawled I, for that is what a beast-boy says when he is chargin souls.

Down the sand a cane were raised what were near as large as the body what helt it.

'Charge!' come the shrill voice of the child as he swung it through the air. 'Charge!'

Out in front, among a cluster of men, were the Stone Thrower, half the size of those what surrounded him. In his fists the cane were helt crossways as he begun runnin twort me. Upon the mug he wore the mask of the Prelate what were loose and jiggled up-a-down upon his skull. Slippin further with each stride the beak were near peckin his chest afore it swung to the side and begun flappin about the shoulder. Takin the mask in hand, he ran with the hooked snout restin in his palm so as it didnoh fall from the skull all agether. He looked fierce dozy, truth be tolt, near trippin over himsen with the cane and mask what were too big and his wee pegs what were too small to carry him through the sand. He were roiled, sure and certain, I'd say the fact he knowt he looked a mooncalf made him more roiled still – if that were possible.

'Charge!' bawled he. 'Kill the Beastht inside the Beastht!'

That were me I sposed. The men begun overtakin him on account of the fact his pegs kep slippin and squelchin in the sand and he were half-blind from the mask wagglin about the skull. When they was near I took up a spear and throwt it hard as I could. It come from the hand flush and made the sound it do when throwt swift and proper – *Woo, woo, woo, woo*, sayt the spear. Flyin straight, it come through the air and caught a soul right in his chest, whereupon he stopped in a sudden, become silent and lay upon the shore. The others took no notice a course, but kep comin all the same.

'Charge!' bawled the Stone Thrower.

I had one spear left, so there were no point throwin it, instead I waited till the men was upon me and – holdin it out with the arm – thrust it into the gizzards of the first gowk I come across, who, unlike his cully, didnoh keep silent but hollered and shrieked like the Devil. I'd the sword raised as well what I drove through the mooncalf next him. Truth were though, I were surrounded by a rake of gowks and there were naught what could be done about it. At near the same spell as I'd plunged the sword into the Grathican, I felt somethin enter my side, from where I couldnoh say, but afore I knowt it I were lyin upon the sand and there were a frenzy of limbs and weapons of all kinds rainin down upon me. I lashed out blind-like; spittin and cursin I grabbed hold of the nearest peg and sunk my teeth into it. Gnawin upon the calf like a rabid dog I yanked the jaw side-a-side, growlin and snarlin and so fort. The soul whose peg I were chompin were none too pleased a course, and he begun kickin and jabbin into me along with the rest. Feelin somethin sharp come through the thigh I growled and hollered but didnoh take the teeth from his skin, instead I bit down harder and let the bitter taste of gowk's blood slide down the back of my throat.

'Halt!' come the command. 'Halt!' sayt he.

The men all stopped and stood back, cep the soul whose leg I were chewin, he kep kickin and hittin me while howlin and carryin-on. He were tryin to beat me off with the gnarled cudgel he wielded in his hand but I had the old lockjaw upon him, so as the more he pounded and prodded me, the harder I bit down upon him.

'Halt, I sayt ye!' shrieked the Stone Thrower, fixin the mask upon his skull as he come through the cluster of men.

The soul whose calf were still betwix my teeth had come to shore and were kickin and lashin at me horizontalwise.

'Geh off! Devil's thrall!' yelped he.

His skull turnt skyward as the Stone Thrower come over him.

'It burns!' sayt he. 'The teeth burn! Get him off, take the Devil from me!'

He were startin to become hysterical, whippin and flailin about and so fort.

Holdin the mask in one hand, the child took a skean from his waistband and drove it through the gullet of the soul whose peg I were gnawin; blood come from there in great spurtin flourishes, keepin time to the pumpin of his heart. I kep my gob wrapped round his calf as death rattled through his bones, his body quakin this-way-a-that in mortal shock. I could feel the death throes through my teeth, mortality tuggin at my gob, pullin me this-way-a-that, strong at first then weaker, till his wiltin wanin soul growt dim and distant afore leavin the world with two faint and final tugs – *tug-tug-tug-tug, tug – tug – tug – tug, tug*. When he become still and calm, I took the gob from his flesh and rolled to the back. Gaspin for air, I stared into a mottled sky encrusted with the dark and dozy skulls of the Grathicans what stood over me. Chucklin some my lips parted, displayin teeth bloody and crimson.

'Let go hathnoh he?' sayt the Stone Thrower to the still and gory soul lyin limp upon the shore.

Hands come across the corpse quick-like and it disappeared behind the cluster of men. The boy come to me then, crouchin over and peerin into my mug.

196

'Thou hast blood on thy hands and can no longer touch the Sacred Stones,' sayt I. 'Thou hast become a man.'

The mask hung slack upon his skull and only one eye could be seen peepin through the glass panels.

'Thou hatht become pale and deathly,' sayt he.

It were the first chance I'd taken forta look down upon mysen and see how I were fairin. The child were right, I were poorly, what with the broken spear comin from the thigh and other bloody and unexplicant perforations. Seein the state I were in somewise brought me back to the body, for in a sudden all the batterin it had taken come floodin through the veins and, truth be tolt, I felt a wee bit sorry for mysen.

'Thou art the Prelate now?' enquizzened I.

'There are things what must be done first – I shall become a man twice afore day's end,' sayt he, risin to the feet. 'Take him back to the Beastht. He shall be slaughtered with hith own kind, their blood shall be contained to that stretch of sand and defile the Quag no further.'

I were taken up in the arms of the gowks – bit rough and hostile for my likin – and hauled across the sands. I spied Withy and Throstle happed up snug and tight in the arms of the gowks what helt em.

'We sayt naught!' bawled Throstle when I caught his eye. 'We sayt naught!'

'Thou hast ventured into the Wastelands unsheeted,' sayt I, lookin him up-a-down.

With a gowk's hand clapped across his gob, Throstle nodded his skull.

'I am to the brim with pride,' sayt I. 'Thou hast showed much fortitude and mettle.'

Withy seemed reluctant to look upon me and I only got a wee glimpse of his bowed and forlorn skull afore the gowks marched off down the sand – a broken overgrowt bairn, cradled in their arms.

Melas had become fierce spirited, bobbin up-a-down to the lopin strides of the gowks what carried me.

Thou looks poorly, sayt she.

'Know that well,' sayt I.

Thou looks like death warmed up.

'Aye.'

Thou looks near as poorly as the whale.

'Ner ye bother bout that!' sayt I, lookin upon her grave and serious. 'I've a thing to enquizzen ye.'

Naught.

'Art thou listenin?'

Aye.

'Listen well,' I tolt her. 'Thou cannoh leave me here.'

Naught.

'Art thou listenin?'

Aye! sayt she. *Impatience itsen thou hast become!*

'Donoh leave me here,' I tolt her. 'Donoh leave Levi and me upon these godforsaken shores.'

She sayt naught to that and I lay back in the arms of the gowks, watchin the sea surge back-a-fort, reachin for the shore and drawin back into hersen – breathin, so she were, and ponderin my request.

As we drew near, the men stopped in their tracks and would go no further, for the butterflies had come away from Levi and begun swarmin round her like wasps.

'Closer!' sayt the child.

The men didnoh move, but stayed where they was, skulls lowered with my pale and poorly sen wrapped and bleedin in their arms.

'Aye! Closer, gowks! Let us all crawl into the belly of the Beast!' whooped I, thrustin mine arm twort the whale. 'Onwards!'

Eyes down and shamefaced, the men didnoh move – the Closemen stood apart some, silent and dreary.

'They'll noh listen to me neither, child, no point botherin with these spineless gowks, let us, ye and I, go fort into the belly of the Beast!'

He took no notice a course, but kep his eye upon the men.

'Closer!' shouted he, pointin with the cane, as though that may help.

Slowise, the men lowered me to the sand, very soft and gentle mind, as though in a sudden I'd become a fragile and delicate thing – *let us be reverent and tender twort this creature we are offerin up for the slaughter.* Very thoughtful souls they was, swear to God. After I were laid upon the shore the men stepped away, washin their hands of me, for they'd come to the conclusion – what werenoh unfounded – that I were a bad business all agether.

'Cowardth!' screeched he. 'Rakes and lechers the lot of ye!'

Comin fort, he placed the cane upon the sand. Takin me by the ankles, he begun draggin me with all he may across the shore twort Levi and the butterflies.

'Pull!' bawled I. 'Pull!'

He stopped and looked upon me when I sayt that.

'Keep thy gob shut, Devil!'

'Pull!'

'I'll close it for ye soon enough,' sayt he, clampin down upon the pegs.

I could see half his seethin and fulminated mug, what with the mask all lop-sided.

'Thy mask has become skew-whiff atop thy skull.'

'Shut it!' sayt he, but fixed it all the same.

'Thy mug has become all puffy and bothered.'

'Yaaaaahhhhh!' bawled he, pullin upon the ankles.

'I am concerned for yer heart.'

He drew back on the pegs, bawlin and hallooin with the effort.

'Pull, child!'

Lettin go of the ankles my legs come thuddin to the shore.

'Mind!' sayt I, wincin with the pain and fixin him with fierce penetratin orbs. 'The pegs have become a wee bit tender of late,' explicant I, grittin the teeth and smilin.

Turnin back, I saw we'd noh come far on account of the fact the child's scrawny arms werenoh strong enough to drag my limp and cumbersome sen. Takin me by the wrists the Stone Thrower spun me round and tried to drag me thatwise.

'I donoh see how this will help,' sayt I.

Truth were though, I liked it better that way, for I were aneath the boy lookin straight up into the mask as he attempted to drag me across the sand with his very agitated and earnest mug. Streaks of the Prelate's blood had dried upon the mask, the tip of the beak were stained red as it flipped and flopped about, half on, half off his skull.

'Yaaaahhhh,' bawled the child, still-yet, we went nowhere.

'Here, let me help.'

Liftin a leg, I begun pushin mysen along with one foot as he tugged upon the arms.

'No!' sayt he.

But I kep goin with the peg, otherwise we'd still be there, me bleedin upon the sand with him pullin the arm near out its socket.

'Nooooo!' hissed he through the teeth.

'Just a little,' hushpered I, very confidential. 'A gentle push or two to see us on our way. We'll tell em ye done it all by yersen – twill be our wee secret.'

'Nooooo!'

There were a quiver in his voice, as though it were about to break. His hands were tremblin too and had become all dank and slippery. The mask come to the side of his mug and I could see there were tears of humiliation runnin down his red and bloated cheeks.

'Pull!' sayt I, but didnoh help with the peg.

Heavin back upon the wrists with all he may, the hands come loose and the Stone Thrower fell backwise.

'Yaaaahh-hah!' sayt he, surprisement joltin his voice as his rump come upon the sand.

With the legs spread afore him, he looked like dejection itsen – a child what had lost its toys, whimperin and wailin upon the shore.

'There, there,' sayt I.

With much wincin, I turnt round and raised mysen upon the elbow.

'Hush now,' sayt I, 'thou hast worked thysen into a flather.'

He remained sittin there upon the sand sulkin and poutin and so fort.

'Think they'll ordain ye Prelate now?' enquizzened I.

He glared upon me with fierce venomous orbs when I sayt that. Pullin himsen agether, he rose to the feet and searched about the sand, for he'd only just minded that he'd brought no weapon. Standin there with the wee chest heavin and shudderin, he fixed his eyes upon the broken spear what protruded slantwise from my peg.

'Thou canst borrow it if thou likes,' sayt I, juttin the chin twort it.

'To the Devil!' sayt he, spittin upon me, afore marchin over to the men.

'I shall wait for ye here!'

Approachin the Closemen, the child tried to reason with em but got no reaction, whereupon he begun wavin and gesticalatin with the arms in frustration. The First Closeman waited for the Stone Thrower to finish afore he shook his skull, lowered his eyes and placed his arms across his body, which were the posture of exile and banishment. Soon after the other Closemen all done the same. The child went to the Grathicans next, approachin one then the other, but the very same happened – skulls shaken, eyes cast to the ground. Rushin fort, the boy snatched a sword from the hands of one of the men and turnt back down the sand.

He were out of breath when he reached me.

'Thou art tired and in need of rest,' sayt I, pattin the sand aside me.

Wrappin both hands round the helve of the sword, the child raised it above his skull, preparin to drive it through me. Truth be, I'd ner seen a soul as distressed as he. Bringin my pegs agether and fixin the arms to my sides, I begun wrigglin and threshin the body about, flippin and flailin upon the shore while the boy helt the sword above me, horror-stricken and repelled. I begun makin noises – lookin the child in the orbs I started to make wee bleatin sounds in the back of my throat like those the calf had made as it were bein butchered afore its mother.

The tip of the blade come back to the shore and the boy lifted the mask atop his skull. His expression were a jumble of confusion and disdain what had turnt his mug all squishy. As I flailed about, wailin and croonin and so fort, I saw the Grathicans start to approach – it were an arrestin sight, I imagine, watchin a beast-boy flippin and wailin and carryin-on as though he were the calf of the Leviathan bein slaughtered upon the damp grey shores of the Quag.

My body landed heavy upon the wet sand; thwackin and slappin agin the shore I keened with all I may till the unhuman cries come strained and trill from my gob. Comin to the side, I kep writhin upon the sand, thrashin the skull upon the shore over and over, till the Quag become muzzy and uneven as though it were the sea itsen. Strange as it may seem to ye, it amused me some to see the world like that, all quivery and liquid. I come down flush upon the side of the skull and heard a poppin sound deep inside the lug. I musta thrashed mysen clear unconscious for next thing I knowt I had become still, and were fierce queasy in the gizzards and dozy in the skull.

There were spatterins and blobs of red from where I'd threshed the skull upon the shore. The Grathicans above were all lookin upon me, havin a proper gawk while I lay there, feelin the body as a chain of wee vibrant and intertwinin torments. Tender and smartin, all I could manage ado were roll onto the back. Raisin the hand to the cheek – what had become rough with blood and sand – I felt a strange numbness on that side of the skull, and slowise I come to fathom that I'd deafened the ear and had rolled into a world what had become silent on one side.

'He is the bairn of the Beastht, the kin of Leviathan! The Prelate were right, and ye all have doubted, ye all have questioned the bloodline that delivered us unto thalvation.'

The boy looked upon the First Closeman, what nodded his skull in accord. This spell the child didnoh hesitate but took a great lungful of air and raised the sword above his skull.

'Thou art cast back to the Hell from which ye have come!' sayt the Closeman.

'Get thee back, Devil! Take thee back to himthen, the Beastht! Yaaahhhhaaaaa!'

Expellin every whit and jot of breath contained in his wee malevolent lungs, the child drove the sword into my chest.

Things become very simple in a sudden, for there were naught in the world cep the passin of metal through flesh – the gelid dark seas bein thrust through my centre. I felt every inch of the cold metal as it come through me, and it spaked to me so it did, I swear upon the Leviathan and her calf the blade spaked to me – *Ye are a thing of the Wastes now, thou hast become a beast true and proper. Wild and free art thou*, sayt the sword, as it flooded mine insides with blood – *No soul can catch thee now.*

The men clustered were all starin upon my pegs with very confused mugs. It were that way I knowt the feet was movin and all – I'd bin tellin em to move, but it were only when I saw their expressions that I knowt sure and certain they was.

'Ahhg thragh arhm,' sayt I.

The Stone Thrower knelt aside me, pressin the lug agin my lips.

'What sayest the Devil for himthen?'

I tried again, but it were a struggle to get my tongue round the words.

'What sayt he?' come a voice among the men.

'Devil-thpake,' sayt the boy, turnin to look upon em.

I raised the skull forta declare, clear and true, my last and final words, for it were important they was understood as they would, no doubt, be cited throughout all eternity.

'Thrum! Thrum! Thrum!' bawled I, blood burblin from my gob as the sea rose in a black and menacin wave over the child's skull – puzzlement crinklin across his forehead as he watched my mug become enveloped in shade.

I worked the pegs best I could as Melas surged twort the shore and a great dozy smile wriggled across the gob. I did the old Thrum-Patter horizontalwise till the skull slumped to the side and the orbs become fixed upon the whale – for it were she a course, what I kep in my sights as the world growt dim, and I become still and mortal.

Melas come lashin agin the shore then – *Whhhooosh!* sayt she, scoopin up shriekin souls and drawin em into her dark bosom while those what could ran for their wee Grathican lives. Drawin back and surgin fort, the sea marched upon the Quag, wrappin her cold black arms good and proper round mysen and the Leviathan forta take us back into her. As my skull bobbed up-a-down slack and lifeless in the water, I watched Levi's colossal sen bein taken slowise into the sea, while the few Grathicans what surrounded bawled and wailed with the limbs flailin this-way-a-that.

Arrrhhh! Donoh forsaken our God-fearin, half-drowned souls, sayt they to His Very Divine and Absent Sen, whereafter they become muffled aneath the waves and silent for allway in perpetuity.

Some clung to the sand like it were their very own mother.

Oooohhhh! they moaned, crawlin out the water, gaspin and weepin for their woebegotted and sorry souls.

205

The yawl I'd taken from the ships had become untethered from its moorins and roved helmless upon the waves. It were off to discover new worlds without me, I spose, lands more amenable to the strange and uncommon ways of a beast-boy such as mysen, though, to be honest with ye, I'd allway knowt no such place existed. Heedless of the compass hidden within its hull, the yawl drifted in a distance as all round Grathicans sobbed and howled amid the slushin of the sea. Mysen and the Leviathan kep silent, our big still eyes starin straight through this world into the next – concentratin hard we were upon the world what cometh without end, amen. Somewise the Stone Thrower had managed to slither free of the water, his voice soundin in a distance, yahooin and hollerin, callin for blood and retribution.

'Back!' he were sayin. 'Back watersome shadow of the Netherworld!'

He'd shout the same from the bottom of the sea, no doubt, if that'd bin his fate. Over top of him, drownin out the high-pitched shrill of the child, come Withy – he were chantin a requiem what swirled round the cliffs and sailed over the turbulent threshin of the salt and dark water. Singin for all he were worth his voice come clear and true, sendin me on my way, guidin me through the sea with song.

His lament growt faint and dim as Levi and I were taken out into the depths, taken to where the sound of havoc and tumult were distant, where it were just hersen wadin in the shimmery darkness aside me, like an untethered blubbersome island upon which no man shall live. Beyond the waves, away from the Quag, Melas were calm and restful, as though it bin the ait and the things of man what had roiled and bothered her. Liltin this-way-a-that, she rocked me back-a-fort like

I were a wee bairn in her arms – which were soothin some, truth be tolt, to my recent mortal sen.

That's us then? enquizzened Levi.

That's us.

Have mercy, sayt she, *what a lot of fuss and bother.*

Aye.

Some rest for us now?

Aye, sayt I, some rest.

The twilight sky become smottled with butterflies – *kitter-katter, kitter-katter, kitter-katter* – for they'd followed us out to sea a course, followed Levi to where the waters become placid and hushed. The welkin were filled to the brim with flitterin wings – a cracklin crawlin vault right from the pages of the Book. I woulda smiled some, lookin up at em, had the gob noh become fixed in a dozy half-opened grimace. From among the flitterin rabble above, one of the creatures withered – foldin its wings it dropped from the sky, whirligigin through the air till its near weightless sen rested, silent-like, upon the sea, where it bobbed up-a-down upon small totterin waves. Another butterfly curled its wings and spiralled to the water, then another and another, till they was droppin from the grey and gloomy sky in droves. Twirlin through the air they covered the surface of the sea – smotherin the darkness with mortal colour what lapped upon the shores of my waned and wilted sen. They fell across mine eyes and covered the lips – they lay upon my chest and become settled and snug agin the pegs and feet. They covered the great mass of her grey and mysterious sen and turnt the water what stretched betwix into a wrigglesome blanket of rickety wings, enfolded and vacillatin upon the waves. It were the weight of their feathery sens what sank Levi and me, like a hand placed soft upon us forta coax us back into the dark and yawnin depths.

I watched the butterflies from aneath the water, bodies crushed agether, pitchin back-a-fort upon the waves and linin the surface of the sea – a marker dividin my world from theirs, a thin place, tracin the distance betwix the livin and the dead. And for all ye who expect lights and a restful eternity, well I hope ye donoh suffer from the sickness of the sea, for I can tell ye that out here there is naught cep the black undulatin waves and the low mournful song of the Leviathan. And fear noh Hell nor damnation neither, for what need be there for em while there are still men on earth. That is the tenth and final decree in *The Philosophy of the Wastelands*, carve em in stone and pass em on to yer weans.

Hersen? ye may well enquizzen. *What has become of her fierce and blubbery sen?* Well, truth be tolt, it were time she and I went our separate ways. Still-yet, as I watched her great body roll away into the murk and dark of the water, I understood that – even afore she come – for allway praps, there'd bin somethin solemn and silent what lay washed upon our shores. A mass, a presence, grey and round and impregnable like a dream. One thing I can say, sure and certain, is that I'd allway felt her lyin across my gizzards, still-yet, noh knowin what she were. She'd bin with me for allway, constant-like, lyin hard and heavy upon me.

Acknowledgements

I would like to express my gratitude to Anne Enright for her encouragement and advice, and without whom there is a fair to middling chance this book would never have been published. Many thanks to Matthew Turner of RCW for reading early drafts, for the work he put into the book and advising restraint when it was needed. Thanks to Sarah Gilmartin, a reader of both early and later iterations of the novel. Many thanks to Becky Walsh and Abigail Scruby for their editorial advice, and to John Murray Originals for providing a space for writing that does not easily fit categories or tick boxes. I am grateful to the Kilkenny Arts Office and the Arts Council of Ireland for their financial support and to Jason Molina, Arthur Russell, Connor Walsh, and Dirty Three for making music and providing refuge. Big thanks to Marian Kilcoyne for all of her support, and the wider Kilcoyne clan for their generosity. Last but not least I would like to thank Angela Ryan who has read almost as many drafts of this book as I have and whose advice, encouragement and opinion, on things literary or otherwise, has always been paramount, thank you kindly for twenty-five years of hell and laughter – Godspeed.

The song 'A Beast Washed Ashore' by White Hinterland provided the armature upon which the world of *She That Lay* was built.

ORIGINALS
NEW WRITING FROM BRITAIN'S OLDEST PUBLISHER

2022

Catchlights | **Niamh Prior**
A 'clever, literary and intriguing' (*Irish Examiner*) novel in stories about shallow and deep acts of cruelty, love, selfishness and kindness which reverberate for years.

Nobody Gets Out Alive | **Leigh Newman**
An exhilarating, 'irresistible' (Jonathan Lee) story collection about women navigating the wilds of male-dominated Alaskan society.

Free to Go | **Esa Aldegheri**
One woman's around-the-world adventure, and an 'honest and perceptive' (Lois Pryce) exploration of borders, freedom and motherhood.

2021

Penny Baps | **Kevin Doherty**
A beautifully-told debut about the relationship between brothers and the difference between good and bad by a 'new, original voice' (*Irish Times*).

A Length of Road | **Robert Hamberger**
A memoir about love and loss, fatherhood and masculinity, and John Clare, by a Polari Prize-shortlisted poet, 'whose work is rooted in people and relationships' (Jackie Wills).

We Could Not See the Stars | **Elizabeth Wong**
Han must leave his village and venture to a group of islands to discover the truth about his mother–'There is really no book quite like it' (*A Naga of the Nusantara*).

2020
Toto Among the Murderers | **Sally J Morgan**
An 'exhilarating' (Susan Barker) debut novel set in 1970s Leeds and Sheffield when attacks on women punctuated the news.

Self-Portrait in Black and White | **Thomas Chatterton Williams**
An 'extraordinarily thought-provoking' (*Sunday Times*) interrogation of race and identity from one of America's most brilliant cultural critics.

2019
Asghar and Zahra | **Sameer Rahim**
A 'funny, wise and beautifully written' (Colm Tóibín, *New Statesman*) account of a doomed marriage.

Nobber | **Oisín Fagan**
A wildly inventive and audacious fourteenth-century Irish Plague novel that is 'vigorously, writhingly itself' (*Observer*, Books of the Year).

2018
A Kind of Freedom | **Margaret Wilkerson Sexton**
A fascinating exploration of the long-lasting and enduring divisive legacy of slavery by a writer of 'uncommon nerve and talent' (*New York Times*).

Jott | **Sam Thompson**

A 'complex, nuanced novel of extraordinary perception' (*Herald*) about friendship, madness and modernism.

Game Theory | **Thomas Jones**

A 'well observed and ruthlessly truthful' (*Daily Mail*) comedy about friendship, sex and parenting, and about the games people play.

2017
Elmet | **Fiona Mozley**

'A quiet explosion of a book, exquisite and unforgettable' (*The Economist*), about a family living on land that isn't theirs.

2016
Blind Water Pass | **Anna Metcalfe**

A debut collection of stories about communication and miscommunication, between characters and across cultures that 'demonstrates a grasp of storytelling beyond the expectations of any debut author' (*Observer*).

The Bed Moved | **Rebecca Schiff**

Frank and irreverent, these stories offer a singular view of growing up (or not) and finding love (or not) from 'a fresh voice well worth listening to' (*Atlantic*).

Marlow's Landing | **Toby Vieira**

An 'economical, accomplished and assured' (*The Times*) novel of diamonds, deceit and a trip up-river.

2015

An Account of the Decline of the Great Auk, According to One Who Saw It | Jessie Greengrass

The twelve stories in this 'spectacularly accomplished' (*The Economist*) collection range over centuries and across the world.

Generation | Paula McGrath

'A hugely ambitious and compelling' (*Irish Times*) novel spanning generations and continents on an epic scale.